## "WIN THIS FACE-OFF
## IF IT KILLS YOU"

Brad whispered the words to his brother as T.J.
positioned himself over the red face-off circle.

T.J. nodded, his face a mask. As Coach Ryan
dropped the puck between Glen and T.J., both
centers lashed at it, with T.J. coming out the
victor. He tipped the puck back to Brad, who
tore across Team B's blue line like a man possessed. Brad feigned to the right, and then
spun around and slid the disk back to T.J., who
he somehow knew would be just behind him.
T.J. let it brush against his stick's blade for a
second, and then blipped the black rubber disk
into the upper left side of the cage, just over
the goalie's shoulder. They continued to get
goal after goal. Playing on a line with T.J. was
like playing with Wayne Gretzky. Brad had almost forgotten that feeling.

# FACE-OFF

## STACY DRUMTRA

AN AVON FLARE BOOK

FACE-OFF is an original publication of Avon Books. This work has never before appeared in book form. This work is a novel. Any similarity to actual persons or events is purely coincidental.

AVON BOOKS
A division of
The Hearst Corporation
1350 Avenue of the Americas
New York, New York 10019

Copyright © 1992 by Stacy Drumtra
Published by arrangement with the author
Library of Congress Catalog Card Number: 92-90566
ISBN: 0-380-76863-1
RL: 6.5

First Avon Flare Printing: November 1992

AVON FLARE TRADEMARK REG. U.S. PAT. OFF. AND IN OTHER COUNTRIES, MARCA REGISTRADA, HECHO EN U.S.A.

Printed in the U.S.A.

RA 10 9 8 7 6 5 4 3 2

**For Mom and Dad
with love**

# CHAPTER ONE

NINE-YEAR-OLD Jory McKendrick's green eyes widened. "Wow, you sure can lift a lot," he marveled as his older brother T. J. began another set of bench presses.

T. J. grinned from beneath the barbell. "You'll be keeping up with me soon enough," he replied. Grunting as he reached ten, he sat up and brushed a sweaty shirt sleeve across his forehead.

"I hope so," Jory replied.

T. J. leaned forward and turned up his Def Leppard tape. "Don't worry, you'll get there. You think Rome got built in a day?"

Jory looked blank. "I don't know."

T. J. sighed. "Never mind. Do you think Arnold Schwarzenegger had muscles that big when he was nine?"

Jory giggled. "No."

"Well, see then."

"Thomas, why aren't you studying? I thought you had a chemistry test today."

Groaning inwardly, T. J. turned to find the grim face of his father looming over him. Six feet tall, with graying chestnut hair and piercing blue eyes,

Thomas Jason McKendrick was a commanding figure whose mere presence was enough to make anyone who crossed him shudder.

"Dad, it's seven o'clock in the morning. Give me a break."

Jory tried to help. "Yeah, Dad, he had to lift weights."

T. J. shook his head. Didn't little brothers know anything? "Great, Jor," he muttered.

"Oh, he had to lift weights, did he? Well surely, Thomas, if you had enough energy to lift weights, you had enough energy to open your chemistry textbook?"

T. J. closed his eyes for a second, and then he stood up. Though he was by no means short, he wasn't quite as tall as his father. But he was the perfect height for a hockey player. "Dad, I studied yesterday. I really don't think a few minutes of cramming—"

"Thomas, this is your junior year in high school. Do you know how closely colleges look at the junior year grades? Every time I see you lately you're thinking about sports. Athletics are fine as extra-curricular activities, but you're not going to get into a school like Harvard if you neglect your studies."

T. J. sighed. "Dad, I don't want to go to a school like Harvard. I've told you."

"You're too young to know what you want. You have so much potential. You could go to any undergraduate school you chose, and go on to law school. But you have to put some effort into it, and lifting weights and playing sports all the time is not the way to go about it."

"Dad, come on. You don't—"

"We'll talk more about this later," his father interrupted, glancing down at his watch. "Now go get ready for school."

"But Dad—"

"I said, enough, Thomas," his father cut in firmly.

Jory, who had been silent for most of the exchange, now tugged at his father's coat sleeve. "Daddy, will you play catch with me tonight?" he asked hopefully. Mr. McKendrick reached down and ruffled his son's silky blond hair. "Sorry, Jor, I'm working late tonight. Maybe tomorrow, okay?"

"Look, I've got to get ready for school," T. J. said. He stalked past his father and entered the bathroom across the hall.

The small blue and white tiled bathroom that T. J. shared with his fraternal twin brother, Brad, Jory, and their thirteen-year-old brother, Chris, seemed even smaller cluttered with the four boys' jumbled belongings. Strewn across the room were Jory's Teenage Mutant Ninja Turtle toothbrush and other turtle paraphernalia, Chris and Brad's Boston Bruins towels, and his own hair dryer, mousse, and styling gel.

Because T. J. was fussy about his appearance and always spent at least ten minutes perfecting his hair before he went out anywhere, his friends had nicknamed him G.Q. But while his vanity was a source of amusement to his friends, to his brothers it was a source of provocation.

T. J. took a quick shower and then got dressed. As he picked up his comb, he was interrupted by a loud hammering at the bathroom door. "T. J., what the heck are you doing in there—having it washed, cut, and blow-dried? Come on."

"Brad, give me a break! I've only been in here five minutes."

"Yeah, five minutes in dog years maybe," Brad shot back.

T. J. was about to retort, when his eyes lit on his red hair dryer. Though his blond hair was only slightly damp, he pointedly switched it on.

"T. J., come on!" Brad shouted, his banging growing more insistent. T. J. let him smolder for another couple of minutes and then flipped off the hair dryer and opened the door.

Brad glared at him, "T. J., if I'm late for school today—"

"Oh, will you chill out already? Man." Smiling to himself, T. J. pushed past his brother and stomped downstairs.

The rest of his family was gathered around the dining room table, his mother and father at either end, and Chris and Jory across from each other. T. J. could feel the tension in the room the second he entered, and he immediately knew the cause of it—his parents had been arguing again. He could tell from the way they were looking at anything but each other and by the redness of his mother's eyes. His anger toward his father returned, and he shot him a sullen look as he circled the table and quietly slid into the chair beside Chris.

"Good morning, T. J." his mother murmured. Forcing a smile, she passed him a plate stacked with lightly browned pancakes.

"T. J., will you drive me down to David's house

after school today?" Chris asked. "We want to go down to the rink and practice our wrist shots."

"I can't, at least not right after school," T. J. replied, forking a couple of pancakes onto his plate. "I've got cross-country practice today. I could take you around four, though."

"I don't know; that wouldn't give me and Dave much practice time. Maybe Brad can take me. You're going into work with Patti today, right, Mom, so the car will be here?"

"Yes, the car will be here, but I think Brad has soccer practice today," his mother reminded him.

"Oh, yeah," Chris said.

"If you go, can I come too?" Jory asked.

"You? You're just a little kid," Chris scoffed.

"So? I play hockey too."

"So I don't want you following me around the whole time," Chris retorted.

"Christopher, what if your older brothers had said that to you when you were Jory's age?" his mother asked. "Who would have introduced you to hockey in the first place?"

"Actually," T. J. commented, grinning, "we did say that to him. The kid just doesn't know how to take a hint."

Chris grinned too. "But I was never that pesty, was I?" He gestured toward Jory.

"You were worse. Compared to you, Jory is nothing."

"Hey, quit talking about me like I'm not here," Jory protested.

"Now, where have *you* been?" Mr. McKendrick asked a few minutes later, as Brad swaggered into the room and took his seat next to Jory.

"I was out jogging," he replied, picking up the orange juice carton and pouring himself a glassful.

As his father smiled, T. J. shook his head. "How many miles today?" Mr. McKendrick asked.

"One and a half. I kind of overslept a little," Brad explained.

Suddenly, the telephone shrilled and Mrs. McKendrick went into the living room to answer it. She returned a moment later and gestured to her husband. "It's Bob."

Mr. McKendrick pushed back his chair. "I'll take it in the study."

"Who's Bob?" Jory asked as his parents left the room.

"Dad's partner," T. J. replied, gazing after his parents.

"Hey, Brad, do you have soccer practice today?"

"Why? What do you want me to do?" Brad asked suspiciously.

"Drive me to Dave's house? Mom said she's not taking the car to work."

Brad nodded slowly. "Yeah, I guess. What are you gonna do at Dave's?"

"Walk down to the rink. I'm gonna help Dave with his wrist shot," Chris said.

"Why? Doesn't he want to improve it?"

Chris glared at him.

Brad grinned. "Just kidding. Meet me at the house around three, and then look for me at the rink around five—maybe I'll give you guys a lift home."

"Really? Are you going to be there too?"

"Yeah, I was thinking about taking Jory." He

turned to his younger brother and saw that his eyes had lit up with excitement. "Hey, how about it, Jor? You want to show me your stuff?"

"Yeah," Jory said eagerly.

A horn suddenly blared outside, and Brad rose and threw on his blue and white Bayview High jacket. "Later, dudes."

As Brad disappeared out the door, T. J. glanced up at the clock. It was already seven-thirty, and his mother hadn't come out to drive his younger brothers to the bus stop. "Listen, guys, I think I'd better take you to the bus today, or you're going to miss it. So go get your books and stuff, okay?"

"How about dropping us off at the movies instead?" Chris asked.

"How about you go get your homework?"

"Well, I would," Chris told him, scrambling to his feet, "except I didn't exactly do it yet."

"Forget it, just hurry up or I'm going to be late for school. How about you, Jory—you got your homework?" T. J. pulled his red and white varsity jacket off the back of his chair and put it on.

Jory nodded and held up a paper covered with scrawled fractions.

"All right, let's split."

The three brothers went out to T. J.'s pride and joy, the second-hand Buick that he had worked two summers as a camp counselor to pay for. It was a silvery blue with a leather interior, a great sound system, and a black and gold bumper sticker on the back that read BOSTON BRUINS #1.

T. J. arrived at the bus stop in the nick of time, just as the mustard yellow vehicle was turning around the corner. After hustling his brothers out of the car, he shifted into drive and burned rubber toward school, all the while trying to ignore the rising speedometer. He broke nearly every speeding law along the way, but he pulled into the student parking lot with perfect timing, just two minutes before the first bell was scheduled to ring.

T. J. hurried among Hayden Preparatory Academy's old and weathered buildings with green ivy clinging to the faded bricks and worn brass plaques mounted above the doors, each bearing the name of the building. Sprawled out over a crisp autumn woodland, Hayden looked more like a traditional New England college than a mere high school.

T. J. bolted into Massey Hall and sprinted down the hallway, skipping his locker altogether and taking the steps leading to his homeroom two at a time.

"Well, if it isn't G.Q.," his friend Tricia teased as he slid into his seat. "Oversleep?"

"This isn't going to be a good day," T. J. replied.

"Why, what's up?" Kevin Mattrex asked from his seat in front of her. Kevin was T. J.'s best friend and his hockey and cross-country teammate, as well as Tricia's boyfriend.

"I had an argument with my father this morning," T. J. said. "He's driving me crazy. All he ever talks about is grades. I was lifting weights, and he started giving me a lecture about studying harder or I won't be able to get into an Ivy League school."

"But your grades are fine," Tricia said.

"Tell him that," T. J. responded.

"He really wants you to go to Harvard, huh?" Kevin asked.

"It's his goal in life."

"Is he the same with all your brothers?" Tricia questioned.

"No, just me," T. J. said. "My brother Brad gets C's, but when he went running this morning my father got this big smile on his face. I'm on the honor roll and he tells me *I* slack off on my homework. Brad's never studied for a test in his life."

"I guess because you've gotten good grades all along, he's resting all his hopes on you," Kevin said.

"I don't know, but I wish he'd quit bugging me," T. J. said.

"What do *you* want to do?" Tricia asked.

"I just want to go somewhere with a good hockey team," T. J. said.

"I'll bet you're getting psyched for the hockey season," Tricia said.

"It's all I've been thinking about," T. J. replied.

"Two more weeks," Kevin said.

"I really want to get captain," T. J. said.

"You'll get it," Kevin replied. "The only guy who even came close to your numbers last season was Todd, and he graduated."

"I hope so. I'm going to the rink after practice tomorrow. Want to go?"

"No thanks. Unlike you, I get tired after practice," Kevin said.

"I'm never too tired for hockey. I can't wait till the games start," T. J. said. "Maybe we'll get some scouts this year."

"After the season we had last year, we should," Kevin said.

"I want to get spotted by an NHL scout more than anything," T. J. said. "I've got to have a good season this year."

"Of course you'll have a good season," Tricia said. "You were All League last year and you were only a sophomore."

"We're going to go all the way this year. I can feel it," T. J. said.

"No more losing in the semifinals like last year," Kevin agreed.

At that moment the principal's voice crackled over the loudspeaker, and the class stood up to recite the Pledge of Allegiance. "So you're not going to the rink with me tomorrow?" T. J. asked Kevin.

"Hey, I'm only concentrating on one sport at a time," Kevin said. "No scouts are gonna come and watch me play."

Grinning, T. J. turned to face the flag.

# CHAPTER TWO

"HEY, MCKENDRICK, YOU been practicing those slap shots?" Brad glanced up from his gym locker to find the large form of his friend and hockey teammate Trey Arenson looming over him. Trey, whose two hundred pounds of hard muscle were spread over an imposing six-foot two-inch frame, looked more like a linebacker than a goalie, but his build made him nothing short of an iron wall in the nets.

"You'd better believe it," Brad responded.

"Think you'll make captain this year?"

Brad shrugged. "I don't know. I hope so."

"It'll be cool if you do. We haven't had a junior as captain since forever."

"Yeah, which makes me even more of a dark horse," Brad said, gathering up his books and snapping his lock shut.

"Gimme a break, McKendrick. Last year you scored more points than all the seniors put together," Trey said.

Brad flashed a grin. "Yeah, I did, didn't I?" he replied as he tried futilely to straighten the loose cover of his chemistry book.

"Modest, too," Trey said, punching his friend's shoulder.

Brad just grinned wider.

"So how do you think you did on Parker's test yesterday?" he asked, as they left the locker room and started down the hall.

"The usual—high D, low C. How about you?"

"I don't know, I actually studied for that one," Brad said.

Trey arched an eyebrow. "Now why on earth would you do a thing like that? You disappoint me, McKendrick. Next thing you're gonna be making the honor roll."

They strolled into their psychology classroom, the first two there.

"Did you see the Bruins' game last night?" Brad asked, sitting down at his desk.

"Yeah. Do you believe that penalty shot?"

Brad started to respond, but then his attention turned to the classroom door. Sherry Taylor was walking into the room. Sherry was new to Bayview, and Brad, who was usually pretty cool around girls, couldn't even work up the nerve to talk to her. Now he found himself staring at her deep blue eyes and the soft blond curls spiraling to her shoulders, and admiring how her black denim skirt and red sweater showed off her tall, slender body.

"I don't get you, McKendrick," Trey said. "Why don't you just ask her out, instead of gaping at her all the time?"

"What are you talking about? I don't gape at her," Brad said defensively.

Trey smirked. "Whatever you say, ace." As their

teacher Mr. Parker ambled into the room, Trey took a seat at the desk behind Brad. He then leaned forward and whispered, "Why don't you take a picture—it'll last longer."

Whirling around and glaring at him, Brad pushed the back of his chair into the front of Trey's desk.

Trey laughed, delighted at the rise he was getting out of his friend. "Nice try, ace. Want me to get a camera?"

"Will you give it a rest, please?" Brad responded.

Mr. Parker, a young man with thick, strawberry blond hair and warm blue eyes, rested his briefcase down on his desk and said, "All right, if Mutt and Jeff back there would kindly tone it down, I'll give you guys a study hall for a few minutes while I finish grading your tests. And let me tell you right now, they leave a lot to be desired."

"Yo, Mr. Parker, did you correct mine yet?" Brad asked.

Mr. Parker chuckled, and some of the seriousness left his face. "No, Brad, and I'm sure you'd like me to keep it that way."

"Hey, you underestimate my abilities," Brad said, feigning hurt. Trey snorted.

Their teacher suppressed a smile. "Now, you can work on homework for another class if you want, but I'd recommend that you start reading chapter three." He grinned wickedly. "You'll like it—it's on Freud."

As the class finally started to simmer down, Brad opened the notebook containing the horror story he was working on and began writing. The words came slowly at first, but within five minutes his pen was flying over the page.

"Hey, what's that?" Trey asked, peering over his friend's shoulder.

Brad closed the notebook. "History homework," he replied.

"Are you sure it's not a love letter?"

"Will you shut up, Trey? You're such an idiot," Brad said.

A few minutes later as Mr. Parker began handing back the psychology tests, Trey commented, "I'm sure this will be something to hang on my wall."

"Not bad," Mr. Parker said setting Brad's test facedown on his desk. Brad flipped it over.

"Ninety-five!" Trey said.

"Good job, Brad. I guess I did underestimate you." Mr. Parker seemed genuinely pleased.

"Well, the test was on abnormal psychology," Trey said. "Don't you think he kind of had an unfair advantage?"

"Trey, shut up," Brad said. Then he started to grin.

Brad drove down the street toward Chris's friend David's house.

" 'Bye, Dave," Chris said shortly, as Brad pulled their mother's station wagon into the Lewinskis' gravel driveway.

David picked up his hockey stick and duffel bag with one hand, and leaned forward and pushed the car door open with the other. " 'Bye, Chris. 'Bye, Jory, and thanks, Brad."

"See you later, Dave." Brad replied absently,

fiddling with the radio dial until he found a decent hard rock station. "And remember, don't look at the puck, look at the players."

"I'm starving," Jory whined as Brad backed out of the driveway and into the street.

"Yeah, me too," Brad agreed. "I wonder what we're having for supper tonight."

Jory made a face. "Meat loaf, I think," he said. But then he brightened, "So do you think my skating is getting any better, Brad?"

"Yeah, you're doing great," Brad told him, reaching over to ruffle his youngest brother's hair.

"Oh, right. He only tripped over the blue line about seven times," Chris grumbled.

Brad glanced back at Chris in the rearview mirror. "You know, you made your share of mistakes when you were nine. What's your problem anyway?"

Chris looked down. "It's nothing," he murmured.

Brad tried to sound offhand. "Did something happen in school today?" he asked.

"I told you, it's nothing!"

Brad raised an eyebrow. "Yeah, well if nothing is bothering you, kid, I'd hate to see you when you're upset about something."

Jory snorted.

"Shut up, Jory," Chris snapped.

Jory sank lower into his seat and was quiet.

A few miles later, as Brad maneuvered the car into their driveway he said, "Jor, why don't you go into the house. I want to talk to Chris for a minute."

Jory got out of the car. "Okay," he replied, "but

hurry up, because I want to play Nintendo with somebody." Grabbing his duffel bag, he ran up to the front door and disappeared into the house.

Brad swiveled around. "So nothing's bothering you, huh?"

"Nope."

"Come off it, Chris."

Chris sighed. "All right. I got into a fight with this kid in school today, and now I have to give Mom and Dad a paper to sign."

Brad frowned. "What happened?"

"Well, I wanted to use the basketball court at recess today," Chris began, "but some other kid took the basketball and wouldn't let me have it, so I punched him."

"You're not in kindergarten, Chris. Couldn't you guys have just played together?"

"I didn't want to play with him. I wanted to play one on one with Jimmy. And besides, I was in a bad mood. I felt like hitting something, and . . . he was there."

"Why did you feel like you wanted to hit something?" Brad asked.

Chris stared out the window. "I don't know. I've . . . felt like that a lot lately."

"And you don't know why?"

Chris nodded.

"Well, next time you feel that way, come and talk to me, all right?"

Chris nodded, and then gathering up his equipment, stepped out of the car. "Here, take Jory's hockey stick," he said.

"You got a broken arm?" Brad replied. Jostling each other, they crossed the grass and entered the house, where they were greeted by the sound of raised voices coming from the den. Their parents were arguing again.

"Oh, no," Chris muttered. He turned to Brad, his eyes wide. "Brad, what am I going to do? I can't give them that note to sign when they're so mad at each other. Dad'll kill me. I'll get grounded for sure." He hesitated for a moment and asked, "Brad, will you sign Dad's name for me? Please?"

Brad sighed. "Chris—"

"Please?" Chris begged.

Brad closed his eyes. "All right, but you've got to promise not to get into any more fights, okay?"

Chris nodded. "Okay."

"Okay, let's have it."

Chris dug into the pocket of his denim jacket and drew out a pen and a folded piece of paper. He glanced around furtively to make sure no one was coming, and then quickly shoved both items over to his brother.

"Remember, Chris, if you get into any more trouble, you'll probably get sent to the principal's office, and we'll both get nailed," Brad said, signing his father's name with a flourish and then handing the paper back to his brother. "So try to control your temper, okay?"

"I will. Thanks, Brad." Chris stuffed the paper back into his pocket and scrambled up the stairs, yelling to Jory.

Shaking his head, Brad switched on the television set and sprawled onto the sofa. What had gotten into his little brother? Chris was a good kid, not the type who went around picking fights. Brad picked up the remote control and began idly flip-

**17**

ping through the channels. He wondered if Chris was upset about all the fighting between their parents lately. If it was tough for him, it had to be even harder on Chris and Jory. Brad promised himself that he'd try to spend more time with both his younger brothers.

Chris and Jory suddenly came bolting down the stairs, Jory holding a Super Mario Brothers cartridge. It was clear where they were headed. "Hey, guys, come on," Brad complained. "I was watching something."

Chris took one look at the TV and then wrinkled his nose. "Give me a break. *The Brady Bunch?*"

Jory was also looking. "Hey, it's the one where Bobby meets Joe Namath!" he exclaimed. "Come on, Chris, let's watch."

Chris stared at both of them like they'd gone nuts. "You guys have got to be kidding me," he said. But seeing he was outnumbered, he pushed Jory aside and lunged toward the armchair.

"Hey!" Jory protested.

"Seniority," Chris said smugly.

As Jory reluctantly settled onto the floor, Brad heard the front door slam, and a moment later T. J. strode into the room. "Hey, guys."

"Hey, Teej," Chris said.

T. J. sank into the couch. "I'm beat. The coach ran us ragged at practice today."

"We have a big game against Westridge tomorrow so we had the day off," Brad said. "There was a pep rally last period. I had to go up to the microphone and talk."

"We have a meet against Mitchell tomorrow," T. J. said. "The coach told me to rest up because

**18**

he's counting on me to win." He picked up the remote control from the coffee table and pointed it at the television.

"That sounds like my coach," Brad said. "I got invited to two parties Friday night." He went on. "I don't know which one to go to."

"I've got one Saturday," T. J. replied. "My friend Craig's parents are out of town."

Suddenly noticing the loud voices drifting from the door, T. J. asked, "How long have they been in there?"

"For as long as we've been home," Brad replied.

"What else is new?" Chris muttered.

T. J. looked at him closely. "So did you teach David that wrist shot?" he asked, changing the subject.

Chris grinned. "Yep, we're going again tomorrow. Want to drive us?"

"What do you think?" T. J. replied.

"Thomas." Brad glanced up to find his father standing in the doorway to the den. "Come into the den for a minute. Your mother and I have something to talk to you about."

"What?" T. J. asked.

"Just come in here."

Brad raised an eyebrow. What was this?

As T. J. brushed by his father and into the den, Mr. McKendrick sighed and raked a finger through his hair. "Listen, why don't you boys go check on dinner?" he said absently. Without waiting for an answer, he put his hand to his head and then went back into the den, closing the door behind him.

# CHAPTER THREE

THE DEN WAS a big bookcase-lined room that also served as Mr. McKendrick's home office. Architectural plans, a protractor, and a compass were spread across the large mahogany desk. The only personal item in the room was a framed snapshot of the entire family in front of Cinderella's castle in Walt Disney World.

The trip had been about five years ago, when T. J. and Brad were eleven, Chris eight, and Jory four. In the photograph, Brad was trying to look cool in a pair of mirrored sunglasses, and T. J.—G.Q. even then—was wearing black jeans with a red bandana tied around the knee, the year's hot look. Chris and Jory were content in denim shorts and matching Mickey Mouse T-shirts, and their parents in sleeveless red tops that read I LOVE FLORIDA.

He had had more fun on that trip than he'd ever had in his life, T. J. thought now. And the Space Mountain incident—he certainly couldn't forget that.

T. J. and Brad had been obsessed with going on Space Mountain almost from the moment the family had started talking about a Florida trip. Their parents had been too old to be interested, or at least T. J. had thought so, and Chris and Jory too young, so while the rest of the family opted for the more sedate spinning teacups, Brad and T. J. had been left to brave the gigantic roller coaster alone. They had to wait in line for something like an hour and a half, and by the time they had finally gotten on, they had been so excited they could hardly walk. By the time they'd gotten off they were still having trouble walking, but now because they were weak kneed and green with nausea. Both brothers had been too stubborn to admit they'd been wrong, so when they'd met up with their family again they had pretended by unspoken agreement that it was the best ride they had ever been on in their lives, and had actually taunted their parents for being too chicken to go on. They had put on a good act, but to this day, neither T. J. nor Brad could hear the words "Space Mountain" uttered without turning a shade greener.

"So what's up?" T. J. asked his parents now.

His mother and father exchanged glances. Finally, his father said, "The situation, son, is that times are tough for architects right now. With the economy in such bad shape, there isn't much building going on and business has been slow." Mr. McKendrick cleared his throat. "What I'm getting at, Thomas, is . . . that I'm afraid we're going to have to cut back some, and we're not going to be able to send you to Hayden anymore."

"What? What are you talking about?" T. J. demanded.

"We're sorry, Thomas," his father replied, "but

we just can't afford private school for you any-more."

"But you can't do this," T. J. protested.

"Honey, believe me, we don't want to," his mother said. "If there was any way we could get around it, we would. But you're going to have to go to Bayview High with Brad."

"But I'm the president of the student council and the captain of the cross-country team! All my friends are there! How do you expect me to start all over again? And what about hockey?"

"T. J. you'll do fine," his mother said, touching his shoulder. "You'll make friends at Bayview."

"Thomas, believe me I wish this weren't neces-sary," his father said. "We don't want to take you out of Hayden. We have to take you out." He paused. "You'll be starting at Bayview at the end of the term."

"But that's next week!"

"T. J.—" his mother said.

"Look, can't I just wait until hockey season is over, and then transfer?"

"Hockey season hasn't even started yet," his fa-ther said.

"But we're going to have a really good team this year. Scouts will probably be coming to our games."

Mr. McKendrick shook his head. "No, Thomas. You're starting at Bayview next week. It can't be helped."

"T. J., Bayview is a perfectly fine school," Mrs. McKendrick told him. "Brad is happy there."

"So?"

"So, if he's happy there, then there isn't any

**22**

reason why you shouldn't be." T. J. stared at the wall. "And Bayview has a good hockey team too," she went on. "You know they made it into the play-offs last year."

He looked at her. "Mom, we were state semifinalists last year!"

"T. J. . . ."

"Look, Thomas, I know you're not happy about this, but you're just going to have to accept it," Mr. McKendrick said.

"Dad, come on! It's not fair!"

"That's enough!" his father said. "And Thomas, even if Bayview isn't as challenging academically, I don't expect you to let your study habits slide. We sent you to Hayden to give you the academic credentials to get into an Ivy League school, not so you could play on a good hockey team."

"My grades are fine!"

"See that they stay that way."

Several minutes later, when T. J. entered the living room, he found Brad and Jory sprawled in front of the TV playing Super Mario Brothers III, and Chris draped over the sofa intermittently watching the game and leafing through an old copy of *Sports Illustrated.*

"What was that all about?" Chris asked, looking up from his magazine.

"Nothing!" T. J. snapped.

"What's the matter with you?" Brad asked.

T. J. threw on his Hayden jacket. "Mom and Dad are making me transfer to Bayview."

"What?" Chris sat up. "What do you mean they're making you transfer to Bayview?"

"I mean they can't afford to send me to private school anymore."

"I'm sorry you have to lower your standards like this," Brad said.

"Shut up, Brad."

"You shut up," Brad replied.

"Hey, this means you and Brad'll be on the same hockey team this year," Chris said.

"Great," Brad said.

"Just what I need—to be on the same team with you."

"At least we agree on something."

"Get lost, Brad."

"Where are you going?" Chris asked as T. J. pulled out his car keys.

"Out," he said shortly.

"T. J.," Mrs. McKendrick protested from the doorway. "T. J., come on, it's time for dinner."

Ignoring her, T. J. went out the front door, slamming it shut behind him.


"I can't believe you're really leaving," Tricia said as T. J. bent down and began scooping his books out of his locker.

"Me either," T. J. said. "I've been going here for four years. All my friends are here. I've known you guys since seventh grade."

"I know, but it's only across town," Tricia said. "We'll still see each other."

"Sure, we'll get together all the time on weekends," Kevin said.

"It's not the same and you know it," T. J. said, piling some books into his duffel bag.

"T. J., you'll make new friends," Tricia said.

"Everybody likes you. And we'll always be here for you."

"Trish, I have to start all over again! You can't just go into a new school in the eleventh grade and make friends. Everyone knows each other. I was in everything here!"

"T. J., it'll be hard but you can do it. You're so smart and friendly that people can't help but like you," Tricia told him. "Just go in with an open mind, and look at it as a way to meet new people. Get involved in things."

"Yeah, at least you'll be starting there right before hockey season starts," Kevin told him.

"What if the guys on the team resent me? My own brother doesn't want me there," T. J. said.

"T. J., of course they'll want you there. Who wouldn't want someone as good as you on their team?" Tricia asked. "You're going to help them win."

"Hey, Teejster." Justin Alexander stopped by his friend's locker. "I'm having a major blowout at my house next weekend while my mom's out of town. Be there."

As he slapped T. J. on the shoulder and disappeared down the hall, T. J. slammed his locker door. "I think I've got bigger things on my mind than partying," he snapped.

"He just doesn't know what to say, Teej," Kevin said.

Glowering, T. J. glared at the wall.

"We're going to miss you, T. J.," Tricia said, reaching over and hugging him. Kevin punched his shoulder and T. J. said, "I'm going to miss you too." Then he turned to face his locker.

# CHAPTER FOUR

"I CAN'T BELIEVE juniors can't even drive to school," T. J. griped, pouring himself a glass of orange juice. "Hayden lets juniors drive to school."

"Too bad, T. J., now you have to live like the common folk," Brad said.

His mother glanced pointedly at Brad before turning to T. J. "It's so nice that Brad's friend Steve is a senior so you can ride with them."

"Yeah. Until you make some friends of your own," Brad grumbled.

"Will you just lay off?" T. J. demanded.

"Just keep out of my space," Brad replied.

"Now, Brad," their mother began.

"Look, don't worry. Other than hockey we have nothing in common," T. J. said. "Unless we end up in some of the same classes, the only time I'm gonna see you if I can help it is on the ice."

"Hey, that's fine with me."

"I wish you two would get along," their mother said.

A horn suddenly blared outside, and Brad scrambled gratefully to his feet. "That's Steve," he told T. J.

Nodding, T. J. threw on his stone-washed denim jacket.

"Now. T. J., all you have to do is stop at the office before the first bell. They should already have your schedule made up for you," Mrs. McKendrick said.

"Okay."

Reaching over, his mother squeezed his shoulder. "Good luck, T. J. I'll be thinking of you."

T. J. smiled slightly. "Thanks, Mom. See you later." Shaking her head sadly, their mother watched as T. J. followed his brother out to Steve's cream-colored Datsun.

Brad climbed into the front seat with Steve, and T. J. slid in back next to Trey and his girlfriend Jessica.

"Why don't you guys just take all day?" Trey complained as Steve pulled away from the curb.

Brad grinned. "And a good morning to you too, Trey."

"Good morning, McKendrick," Trey recited.

Brad introduced T. J. to the kids in the car. Jessica, a petite blonde who was the cocaptain of the cheerleading squad, asked, "Do you know what courses you're taking yet, T. J.?"

"Yeah, I signed up for chemistry, trig, English lit., psychology, and history," T. J. replied.

"Uh oh, better hope you don't get the Dragon Lady for trig," Trey said.

"The Dragon Lady?"

"Old lady Adams. If you get her, transfer. I cannot stress that enough."

"T. J., I've seen you play hockey," Jessica said.

"You're really good. Are you going out for the team this year?"

"Yeah, definitely."

"Then you'd better get acquainted with Steve up there," Trey commented. "If you make the first line, he'll probably be your left winger."

"Why, are you a center?" Steve, a tall dark-haired boy, asked T. J.

"Only in the sense that Wayne Gretzky and Mario Lemieux are centers," Trey answered. "Haven't you ever seen this guy play? He scores goals like Pacman eats power pellets."

"I don't know, I think I might have had the flu the last time we played Hayden. I have heard of you though," Steve told T. J.

"Yeah, me too," T. J. responded. "I saw you play in that game against Lincoln last year, when you scored the hat trick."

"The only hat trick I got all year," Steve said. "So how many goals did you score last season?"

"Thirty-four, I think."

Trey whistled. "Man, you just missed Brad by like two or three, didn't he, Brad?"

Brad stared sullenly out the window, and as Jessica asked T. J. if he had gotten the MVP last year, his jaw tightened.

"Wow, you got it when you were only a sophomore?" Jessica asked.

"Yeah."

"Trey, do we have a psych test today?" Brad asked suddenly.

"That's it, Brad, just change the subject," Jessica said.

"You're a big help," Brad said.

Trey's eyes widened. "Oh, my God, do we?"

A few minutes later, as they entered the crowded Bayview parking lot, Jessica said, "Well, good luck, T. J." She slung her pocketbook over her shoulder. "I hope you're in one of my classes."

Steve smiled. "This must be like starting eighth grade all over again, huh?"

"I hope not. In eighth grade, it took me half a semester to find my locker, never mind all my classes."

Steve laughed. "Well, if you need any help getting to a class or something, just let me know," he said, switching off the ignition. "You can usually find me hanging around the band room."

"That's great, Steve," Trey rejoined. "What's he supposed to do, ask someone where the band room is so he can ask you where his classroom is?"

"Very funny." Steve pushed open the car door. "Hey, T. J., will you need a ride home?"

"Yeah, that'd be great. Thanks, Steve," T. J. responded, stepping out of the car.

Bayview looked nothing like Hayden. Brad thought the two-story tan brick L-shaped building was ugly. But the freshly mowed football and baseball fields sparkled in the early morning dew, and in the distance T. J. could see the newly renovated hockey rink, raising his spirits a little.

"Good luck, T. J.," Trey said as they entered the building. "I'll see you later. See you in psych, Brad."

Brad nodded unenthusiastically.

" 'Bye, T. J.," Jessica said. Trey put his arm around her and they sauntered down the hall.

"Brad, where's the office?" T. J. asked, looking around the jammed hallway.

"End of the hall," Brad said shortly. "Hey, Steve, wait up!"

Later that morning, as Brad was drawing a book out of his locker, he saw Sherry Taylor opening hers further down the hall. No one was around her, and brushing her hair behind her shoulder, she slid a book onto the top shelf. Brad hesitated and took a step in her direction, but then turned back to his locker.

"Brad, your brother is so nice," a familiar voice suddenly exclaimed by his side. Startled, Brad glanced up into Jessica's smiling face.

"Yeah, I guess," he said doubtfully, "if you're talking nice as opposed to an ax murderer or something."

Jessica gazed at him thoughtfully for a moment, and then said, "You and T. J. don't get along too well, do you?"

"You might say that," Brad replied.

Jessica smiled faintly and then said knowingly, "It's because you're so much alike."

Brad snorted. "Me and T. J.? Alike? Yeah, that'll be the day."

"No, I'm serious, Brad. I was just talking to him in trig and he reminded me so much of you."

"We're talking about T. J. McKendrick, right?" Brad asked.

Jessica punched his shoulder. "Brad, just listen for a minute," she urged. "I mean, I thought you and Trey were alike, but T. J. leaves Trey in the dust. He's probably more like you than anyone you know."

"Jessica, T. J.'s nothing like me," Brad said.

"Come on, Brad. He's competitive like you are, he's hardworking, he's smart, he has a good sense of humor," Jessica said. "Tell me that's not like you."

"First of all, I work a lot harder than T. J. does," Brad said. "Everything comes easy for him. And second, everyone who plays sports is competitive. That doesn't mean a thing."

"Brad, you're twins. You're bound to be something alike."

"Look, Jessica, I don't know what you're talking about. T. J. and I are nothing alike."

"I'll bet he's stubborn too," Jessica said.

"You and your sister are both cheerleaders, but that doesn't mean you're alike," Brad said. "I think if someone gave you a gun and told you to shoot her, you'd just turn around and ask how many bullets."

"That's different. My sister's a jerk," Jessica explained.

"So's my brother," Brad replied.

"Brad! If anyone else had said that to you, he'd be pinned to the floor right now."

"Jessie, lighten up," Brad said impatiently. "I was just kidding."

"I hope so, Brad," Jessica said. "I'll see you later, okay?" She disappeared into the throng of students.

Brad tossed his chemistry book into his locker and, banging the door, strode down the hall.

# CHAPTER FIVE

IT HAD BEEN the worst day of T. J.'s life. First, the school secretary hadn't been able to locate his schedule, then he'd been given the wrong locker combination, and now he was totally and completely lost. He felt like a mouse looking for a small wedge of cheese in a giant maze, first down one corridor, then up another. And Trey sure hadn't been kidding about the Dragon Lady; when T. J. had walked in late for trig that morning, Mrs. Adams had been so irate that T. J. had almost expected her head to start spinning around like Linda Blair's in *The Exorcist*.

T. J. glanced around helplessly. The hallway was nearly deserted, except for an eighth or ninth grade boy drinking out of the water fountain and a pretty blond girl getting something out of her locker. T. J. hesitated. He hated asking for help of any kind. An old girlfriend of his had once told him that he was the macho type who would rather drive around in circles for an hour than stop at a gas station for directions, and T. J. had to admit that she was probably right. Reluctantly he approached the girl at the locker.

"Hi. Could you tell me where room nineteen is?"

The girl smiled and closed her locker. "Yeah, I was just on my way there myself. Psychology with Mr. Parker, right?"

T. J. nodded, relieved. "Right." As the clanging of the bell suddenly reverberated throughout the empty halls, T. J. sighed.

"Oh, don't worry about that," the girl assured him. "Mr. Parker won't mind. And besides, he's usually late himself.

"So are you new here?" she asked, as they started down the corridor.

"Yeah. I just transferred over from Hayden," T. J. replied.

"I'm kind of new here myself," she said. "What's your name?"

"T. J. McKendrick."

"Really? Any relation to—"

"Yeah, he's my twin brother," T. J. said shortly.

"I guess you've been getting a lot of that lately, huh?"

"People asking me if I'm related to Brad? Yeah, you could say that," T. J. admitted.

"So, are you a big sports hero too?"

T. J. grinned again. "I like to think so."

"Yeah? What do you play?"

"You name it, I've played it. But hockey is my best," T. J. told her. "And my favorite."

"Really? Who's your favorite player?"

"Brett Hull."

"Yeah, my favorite is Steve Yzerman," she said.

T. J. raised an eyebrow. "Yeah, he's one of mine too. So you follow hockey?"

**33**

"Yes, I follow hockey," she replied. "Why does everybody say that?"

"I was just surprised. I mean, most of the girls I know think hockey players are just a step above Freddy Krueger or somebody."

"They just don't appreciate blood and gore," the girl said with a smile. "Seriously though, I don't like all the fighting, but I don't think it's the big megaproblem that some people make it out to be."

"No kidding," T. J. agreed. "And if they'd just watch a game, they'd know that. I mean, most of those same people couldn't tell you what icing or a power play was if their lives depended on it."

"Yeah, they probably think icing is just something you do to a cake," the girl said. "Well, here we are," she announced, halting in front of a classroom. She pointed through the glass window. "And there's Mr. Parker, just opening up his attendance book."

"Hey, what's your name, anyway?" T. J. asked.

"Sherry Taylor. Oh, and did I tell you that your brother's in this class?" she asked as she opened the door.

Great, T. J. thought, walking in. The room was large and cheery, with the desks arranged in a zigzag format and bright posters covering the walls. One that T. J. especially liked was of a huge white mansion encircled by cars like Ferraris and Porsches; underneath it read "Justification for higher education." Notes on the id, ego, and superego were sprawled across the black chalkboard, and a couple of fliers announcing essay contests and scholarship competitions were pinned to the red-papered bulletin board.

As Sherry slipped into her seat, T. J. went over to talk to Mr. Parker. "Hi. I'm T. J. McKendrick. I just transferred to your class."

Mr. Parker glanced up from his green attendance book and smiled. "Hi, T. J. Welcome to Bayview. How's the day been going for you? You get lost yet?"

"Only before every class," T. J. said.

"Well, don't worry. You'll get used to it. Were you taking a psychology class at your previous school?"

T. J. nodded. "Yeah."

"About what topic did you get up too?"

"We just finished a chapter on Freud," T. J. said.

"Good, you're ahead of the game then. We just started Freud. Why don't you go grab one of those orange books off the back shelf over there, and then take a seat wherever you want. The empty ones in front are pretty much taken, but most of the ones in back should be free."

"Okay, thanks."

"Oh, do you want to be spared the embarrassment of having me introduce you to the class, or doesn't that bother you?"

T. J. laughed. "I think I've sustained enough embarrassment for one day."

"Good choice. By the way, are you related to Brad McKendrick?"

Probably for the tenth time that day, T. J. replied, "Yeah, he's my brother."

"Really?" Mr. Parker asked in surprise. "Oh, of course, you must be the hockey player from Hayden," he remembered. "Well, that should work out perfectly for you. He can give you the notes you've missed."

Yeah, perfect, T. J. thought. As he started for the back of the room, he spotted Sherry sitting up front and Brad and Trey in their letter jackets in the rear. Brad, who was slouched down in his seat, was staring absently out the window, and Trey, who looked equally bored, had his chin resting in one hand and was doodling idly on the inside of his notebook cover with the other. However, he brightened when he saw T. J.

"Hey, T. J., how you doing?" he said. He gestured to the chair beside him. "Sit here."

Brad's eyes narrowed, and as T. J. set his books down on the desk, he slammed shut his psychology book.

"The orange book, right?" T. J. said.

Trey lifted up a corner of his Bart Simpson book cover. "Yep, it's orange all right."

T. J. walked over to the back shelf and returned a moment later with the book. As he sat down, he glanced over at his brother. "Hey, Brad."

"Hi," Brad said coolly.

Mr. Parker rose from his chair and began sweeping the eraser across the blackboard. "Sherry, seeing as you were so late to grace us with your presence today," he remarked over his shoulder, "Why don't you review what we went over in class yesterday?"

The time passed quickly. Mr. Parker was a good teacher, and the atmosphere in the class was warm and relaxed. Before T. J. knew it, the final bell was ringing and the kids were filing out of the classroom. He couldn't believe it—the day was finally over.

As T. J. followed Brad and Trey out the door and into the hallway, a high-pitched voice suddenly asked from behind him, "Excuse me, but aren't you Tommy McKendrick?"

T. J. turned, to find a short dark-haired boy leaning against the locker beside him. Slender, with steel-rimmed glasses and a pimply face, he was familiar somehow, but T. J. wasn't sure why.

"Yeah, except I go by T. J. now."

"I thought it was you," the boy said triumphantly. "It's me, Randy. Randy Keller."

T. J.'s eyes widened. "Randy, God, it's been ages," he said. "How're you doing?" Randy Keller had been T. J.'s best friend from about the third to seventh grade, but T. J. hadn't seen him since he'd transferred to Hayden.

"Fine, how about you?"

"Pretty good," T. J. replied.

"Listen, do you need a ride home?" Randy asked. "It's no trouble, my sister and I go right by your street."

"Oh, thanks, but I already have a ride," T. J. said. "I appreciate it though."

"So how did you like psychology?" Randy asked as he and T. J. walked down the hall and to T. J.'s locker.

T. J. grabbed his jacket and then closed the door. "Well, it was the best class I had today," he replied, continuing down the corridor.

Randy pulled open the side door. "Don't you think Mr. Parker is just a little too informal though?" he pressed.

"I don't know, he seems okay," T. J. responded.

They were silent as they crossed the parking lot. "I don't get it," T. J. said, halting before the space where Steve's car had been that morning. "They were right here."

"Maybe they left already," Randy said.

T. J. looked around. "They were right in front of me when we left psych."

"Well, if you want a ride home with us, it's no problem."

T. J. glanced around the parking lot again. Finally he said, "Yeah, okay."

Five minutes later though, T. J. was cursing himself. All Randy talked about was how high his GPA was, and how he was the president of this and the treasurer of that. He was so full of himself it was sickening. T. J. couldn't get over how drastically his old friend had changed.

" 'Bye, T. J. See you in psych tomorrow," Randy said as his sister pulled into the McKendricks' driveway.

Not if I see you first, T. J. thought silently. After thanking them for the ride, he entered the house, surprised at how angry he felt. Loud heavy metal was pounding from upstairs, and setting his jaw, T. J. mounted the staircase. "Thanks so much for waiting, Brad," he said, slamming the door to Brad's room with a thud.

Brad, who was on the floor doing inclined sit-ups against his bed, glanced up. "Didn't anyone ever teach you to knock?"

"Why didn't you wait?"

"We did wait, man. You just never showed up."

"Give me a break! You knew I'd be there."

"How would I know?" Brad asked. "I thought you must have gotten a ride with your old friend Randy."

"Wait a minute. You must have heard me tell Randy that I already had a ride," T. J. said.

"Yeah, T. J., like I really waste time listening to your conversations," Brad shot back.

"Shut up, Brad."

"You shouldn't be relying on my friends for rides anyway! Get your own."

"Well, just give me a chance to make some!"

"I was giving you a chance to make one!"

"Yeah, right! You left me with Randy because you were trying to help me? You just stuck me with him because he's a geek!"

"Yeah, well, take what you can get, T. J.," Brad said.

T. J. shook his head. "Forget it, Brad, just forget it, all right?" His teeth clenched, he stormed out of the room.

"T. J., can I talk to you for a minute?" Folding over a corner of a page of his English lit. book, T. J. closed the book and looked up from his desk. "Hey, Chris, what's up?"

Hesitating, Chris shut the door and shuffled over to his brother. Staring at the floor, he said, "It's just that . . . I got into this fight in school today, and the principal gave me a thing for Mom and Dad to sign. I was wondering if . . . maybe you'd sign it for me?" He cautiously raised his head.

T. J. couldn't believe it. "You mean you want me to forge Mom and Dad's signatures?" he asked.

"Please, T. J., if they find out they might ground me before hockey season starts," Chris begged.

T. J. sighed and then asked, "Look, before we go any further, why don't you tell me what this fight was about?"

Chris looked away. "But you'll think it's stupid."

T. J. reached over and flipped off his stereo. "Try me."

Chris shrugged his shoulders. "All right, there was this kid at school, Jeff Hall, and he was saying stuff like how he was going to be the starting right wing on the hockey team instead of me, and how I'd be lucky if I even made the team. So I punched him," he concluded matter-of-factly. "Didn't even get a skinned knuckle," he added proudly.

"Yeah, but, Chris, it sounds like he was just jealous of you. Did you really have to hit him?"

"Wouldn't you have?" Chris asked.

"No, I just would've tried doubly hard to leave him in the dust at hockey practice. You admit yourself it was stupid."

"I didn't say it was stupid, I just said that you'd probably think it was stupid," Chris corrected him. "So will you sign it for me?" he asked.

T. J. sighed, and stared at the ceiling. "All right," he said after a moment, "but I mean it, Chris, try to control your temper, okay?"

Chris nodded. "Thanks, T. J.," he said in relief.

T. J. flashed a grin. "And if we get caught, it was Brad that signed it, got it?"

"Got it." As Chris was reaching into his pocket for the form, someone knocked lightly on T. J.'s

**40**

door. Chris's eyes widened, and he jumped like a startled rabbit.

"Chris, calm down," T. J. said. Flicking his stereo back on, he reopened his English text and called, "Come in."

The door swung open and Mrs. McKendrick entered the room, still in her starched nurse's uniform. "Hi, guys. How was your first day of school?" she asked T. J.

T. J. grimaced.

She smiled wryly. "That good, huh?"

"I don't know. I guess it was okay," T. J. admitted, fiddling with a pencil, "but the stupid office couldn't find my schedule so I missed my first class. They had to make me up a whole new schedule."

"Oh, that's too bad," his mother sympathized, "but I guess on the first day of anything you kind of have to expect something to go wrong. Let me give you two a word of advice: no matter how much you want them to, first days will never go smoothly."

"So what's the advice?" T. J. asked.

His mother gave him a look. "But how were your classes? Are your teachers nice?"

T. J. shrugged. "Yeah, I guess they're all right. Except for my trig teacher."

"Who's your trig teacher?" his mother wanted to know.

"Mrs. Adams?"

"Ah, the Dragon Lady," Mrs. McKendrick said knowingly. "I don't know why you kids don't like her. She seemed very nice at the parent-teacher conferences last year."

41

"Well, she has to act nice in front of parents," T. J. told her.

His mother smiled and shook her head. "Well, I suppose I'd better get started on dinner. How do Chinese chicken wings sound?"

"Good, but Dad hates those," Chris said.

"Yes, well, Dad won't be eating with us tonight," his mother replied absently. She rested a hand on T. J.'s shoulder and then left the room.

"Okay, let's see it," T. J. said once he and Chris were alone.

"Thanks again, T. J.," Chris said gratefully, as he drew the form out of his pocket. "You won't regret it, I promise."

"Yeah, well I'd better not," T. J. warned him, taking the paper and carefully signing his mother's name. "Just try not to let things like that get to you. People like that Hall kid aren't worth your getting suspended from school or something, you know?"

"Yeah. I know," Chris said.

T. J. stared at him for a moment, and then said, "Look, if you ever want to talk to me about anything, let me know, okay?"

Chris nodded.

T. J. stood up and grinned. "So how about a game of Nintendo ice hockey?"

Chris pretended to be aghast. "What? And kick out Brad and Jory?"

T. J.'s grin turned wicked. "Yeah, now we've definitely got to play, huh?" As his younger brother smiled, T. J. clapped an arm around Chris's shoulders and followed him downstairs.

\* \* \*

"So T. J., how are things going at school? Have you had any tests yet?" Mr. McKendrick asked a few days later, sinking down onto the couch beside his son.

"Yeah, chemistry," T. J. replied, glancing up from his issue of *Hockey Illustrated*.

"How did you do?"

"Pretty good. An eighty."

"An eighty? What did you get wrong?"

"I don't know, there were a few things the teacher asked that weren't in the book," T. J. replied. "They must have been from notes that he gave before I transferred."

"Well, couldn't you have gotten the notes from someone in the class?" his father asked.

"Dad, I did!" T. J. said. "How am I supposed to know who takes good notes? And an eighty is not exactly bad for coming into a class three days before the test."

"I'm not disputing that, Thomas. I just want to make sure that you don't start coasting now that you're not in private school anymore. If business doesn't pick up, you may have to get a scholarship for college now."

"Hey, Dad," Brad said, coming down the stairs, "can—"

"In a minute, Brad, I'm talking to your brother."

Sighing, Brad went back upstairs.

"So don't let those study habits slip," Mr. McKendrick said, turning back to T. J.

"Dad, I'm not. Look, I was thinking. Maybe I could get a hockey scholarship to BC or someplace," T. J. said.

"A hockey scholarship! I haven't been sending

**43**

you to private school all these years so you could go to college to play hockey! You should be concentrating on your grades."

"Hey, a hockey scholarship pays the bills just like an academic scholarship," T. J. said with a shrug.

"I think Harvard and Yale will be a little more interested in your grade point average than in your hockey totals!"

"What's the matter with BC?" T. J. asked.

"BC is fine for someone who doesn't have the grades that you do," his father replied. "But you could get into any school you want."

"Well, maybe I want to go to BC. It's a perfectly good school."

"I know, but I also know why you want to go there," his father responded. "Because of the record of their hockey team!"

"So, I happen to love hockey!"

"You don't go to college to follow a hobby."

"It's not a hobby!"

"Thomas, you're not Jory's age. You're not going to be a professional hockey player."

"You don't know. You can't foresee the future. I feel that I'm a good enough player that if I can get a scholarship to a college with a good hockey program, I'll have a chance at it."

"Well, what if you don't get a scholarship?" his father demanded. "I'm not paying for you to go to college to play hockey."

"Fine, then I'll go right into pro hockey and I won't have your precious college education at all."

"That's just nonsense, Thomas. I don't want to talk about it any further!"

"That's okay with me. You never listen to what I say anyway." Slamming his magazine down on the table, T. J. stalked out of the room, leaving his father gaping behind him.

# CHAPTER SIX

"HEY, THERE'S T. J.," Steve said to Brad the following afternoon at lunch. "Hey, Teej, over here!" They were at the table with a bunch of their friends.

T. J. set his tray down on the table. "Hey, Steve, what's up?"

"Hi, guys," Sherry Taylor said from behind him, placing her tray beside T. J.'s. As she sat down, Brad glanced from Sherry to T. J.

"Brad, how did you do on the algebra test?" Sherry asked, sipping her milk from a straw.

"Sixty. I bombed it," Brad replied.

"Yeah, I got a fifty," Sherry said. "Thank God for T. J. He's going to tutor me for the next one." She turned to T. J. "You're so smart, T. J. It takes you two minutes to do a problem that I probably couldn't do at all."

"Well, math's my best subject," T. J. responded. "It's English that I have trouble with."

"Yeah, it's the opposite with me," Sherry said. She grabbed a French fry off T. J.'s plate and grinned as he tried to snatch it back. "If you ever need any help in English let me know."

"There is something actually," T. J. told her. "We have to write an argumentative essay."

"Have you started it yet?"

"Yeah, but I don't know if it sounds strong enough."

"Well, let me read it when you come over tonight."

Brad tore open his milk carton and swore as a small puddle spilled onto the table.

"What's the matter with you?" Steve asked.

"Nothing," Brad snapped. Glaring at T. J. he stood up to get a napkin.

Coach Reynolds was short and stocky, with a sagging pouch of a stomach, a drooping walrus mustache, and a shiny dome of a bald head. It was rumored that he had once spent a season with the New York Rangers, but even though it would have been about twenty years ago, Brad still found the picture difficult to imagine. The idea of his burly coach prancing around Madison Square Garden on ice skates just made him burst out laughing.

It was the first hockey practice of the season, and all the kids were clustered together in the bleachers of the Bayview rink, awaiting Reynolds's annual pep talk. "All right, for those of you who haven't played for me before," Reynolds began, hitching up the waistband of his sweatpants, "I'm Coach Reynolds and this is my assistant, Coach Ryan." He gestured beside him to a small birdlike man with glasses. "Here's the drill. We're going to have a week of tryouts, and for those of you who make the cut, an added two and a half weeks of preseason. During those three and a half weeks,

**47**

we'll be running two practice sessions a day. The first will run from six-thirty to seven-thirty in the morning and will be spent weight training, running, and conditioning. The second will last from two-fifteen till about four, and that will take place on the ice. There will be only one practice session on Fridays, the afternoon one at the rink. The practices before games will usually be very light, with mostly scrimmaging and drilling in your weaknesses. I will be making you up a practice schedule, so if you're confused, don't worry about it. Besides regular games, we'll also be playing in a couple of tournaments, including the Christmas tournament coming up in the middle of December, shortly after our first game. I run a tough team, and if you don't intend to work, I'm telling you right now, this team has no place for slackers." As he crossed his arms across his bulging chest, Brad and Trey exchanged knowing glances—now came the pep talk.

"Now I want you guys to remember something. As long as you're on this team, the other guys aren't just your teammates. They're your family. I don't care if you hate each other in school; when you're on the ice, you're one unit. You're not competing against each other, you're competing with each other. And don't try to showboat. Assisting is just as important as scoring." Reynolds cleared his throat. "Now I can't say anything for sure, because I haven't seen all you guys play yet, but with guys like Brad, Trey, Steve, and T. J. on our side, we have the backbone for a very strong team. As you'll recall, last year we almost made it into the state semis, and though we did lose a few key players to graduation, if you all work together and give it everything you've got, there's no reason why this year we can't make it even further." He clapped his hands together. "Okay, now let's hit the ice."

"Great, another McKendrick," Brad heard a sour voice grumble as he began to climb down from the bleachers. "Well, if he thinks he's gonna get first line center, he's in for a major surprise."

Brad whipped his head around. As he had suspected, the sneering voice belonged to Glen McCann. Last year, Brad had been the right wing to Glen's center, and the two had been at each other's throat through the whole season. Glen had continually claimed that Brad never passed, only shot, and that Brad thought he was a one-man show. These accusations had infuriated Brad. Sure, he did shoot slightly more than he passed, but that wasn't showboating; that was instinct. There were times when you should shoot and times when you should pass, and Brad's philosophy was that if you had an open shot, why pass? The rest of the team apparently agreed with him. The only people who seemed to think he was a hotdogger were Glen and his lackey Michael Neved, the defensive forward whom Glen was addressing now.

Brad was about to fire back a retort, when T. J. snapped from behind Glen, "What, are you scared, McCann? Afraid that I'm going to get your position? Well, from what I saw last year, you should be."

Brad started to smile. So much for the coach's one big happy family pep talk. And he wasn't about to let Glen get off without adding his own two cents. "Hey, McCann," he said, "why don't you worry about not tripping over the blue line, and let my brother and me worry about the scoring, okay?"

"Yeah, in your dreams, maybe, McKendrick," Glen said. With a look at Michael, he turned and stalked angrily past them.

T. J. glanced at Brad. "Are they always so pleasant?" he asked.

"Only on good days," Brad replied. "Do you think it's a penalty to hit your own teammate?"

T. J. grinned. "Probably, but maybe we can stick a rusty nail in his skate or something."

Brad was surprised at how good it felt to joke with T. J., just like when they were kids, before they were at each other all the time.

"Hey, guys," Reynolds said, ambling over to them from behind the bench. "T. J., I just wanted to tell you, it's nice to have you on the team. Here's to a good season like last year, right?" He slapped T. J. on the back, and then blew sharply on his whistle. As T. J. skated out to center ice, Brad glared at him, and tightening his grip on his hockey stick, skated past him.

"All right, laddies, ten sprints up and down the length of the ice!" Reynolds called. "And let's hustle."

A few moments later, having finished the sprints before most of his teammates, Brad skated over to the bench and grabbed his water bottle off the seat. Tiny beads of perspiration were glistening on his brow, and his breath was coming out in short, rapid puffs. As he removed his helmet and sucked the straw between his lips, Reynolds shouted,

**50**

"What are you people, old ladies or varsity hockey players?"

A couple of minutes later, once the remaining players had straggled over to the bench, the coach said, "Well, I can see we're gonna have to do a lot of running tomorrow. Now Trey and Sage, take the goals. The rest of you are going to practice your shooting technique." He divided them up with his fingers. "You guys—" he pointed toward Brad, T. J., and about eight others "—you go against Trey. The rest of you I want against Sage. Take two shots each, and then skate to the back of the line. And shooter, stay near your blue line—don't swoop in on your goaltender. You're just practicing your aim."

On his side, Brad was up first, since nobody else wanted to be. Drawing back his heavily taped Titan hockey stick, he slammed a hard slap shot across the ice that Trey deflected easily off his battered goalie pads. Brad grimaced. It was true that this was a difficult position to shoot from, but he had been practicing from that spot for the past week, forcing Chris to play goal. Setting his jaw, Brad slapped his stick against the puck and watched as it sailed down the ice and into an open corner of the net.

"Hey, McKendrick, what are you trying to do, make me look bad?" Trey demanded. Though his tone was light, Brad knew how much his friend hated to give up goals, and he began to feel a little guilty. However, when Coach Ryan yelled out, "Nice shot, McKendrick," Brad grinned.

They continued for another ten minutes, with only T. J. and Brad succeeding in getting the puck past Trey. Once that drill was completed, Reynolds had them run through a couple of passing drills, and after that, skate in and out of pylons. Finally, he blew his whistle and yelled, "Okay. For the last twenty minutes or so we're going to scrimmage. Ordinarily, we'll only scrimmage once or twice a week, but today I need to get an idea of your strengths and weaknesses in game situations. Sage and everyone who shot against Trey in our first drill is Team A, and Trey and everyone who shot against Sage is Team B. Okay, now Team A, raise your hands." As the hands shot up, Reynolds glanced down at the clipboard his assistant was holding. "Okay, T. J., take center, Brad and Steve, right and left wing, and Russ and Mark, defense." Brad noticed Glen shooting T. J. a dirty look, probably because Reynolds had T. J. positioned on Glen's old line. "For the second shift, I want Brett at center, Mike at left, Tony at right and Jim and Doug on defense." He looked down at the clipboard again. "All right, Team B. Glen, center, Matt left, Cory right, Danny and Kirk back; second shift—Will, center, Greg right, Ron left, and Bobby and Max back. The rest of you I'll sub in as needed. Okay, get out there." He reached into the pocket of his satin Celtics jacket and handed Ryan a couple of pucks.

Dropping on his helmet, Brad skated over to the red face-off circle and took his place to the right of his brother. "Win this face-off if it kills you," he murmured to T. J., as Glen positioned himself opposite them.

T. J. nodded, his face a mask. As Coach Ryan dropped the puck between Glen and T. J., both centers lashed at it, with T. J. coming out the victor. He tipped the puck back to Brad, who tore across Team B's blue line like a man possessed. Brad feigned to the right, and then spun around and slid the disk back to T. J., who he somehow knew would be just behind him. T. J. let it brush against his stick's blade for a second, and then flipped the black rubber disk into the upper left side of the cage, just over Trey's shoulder.

Brad and his brother combined for five more goals like that, and in ten minutes the score was Team A, 6, Team B, 1; B had scored when the McKendrick line was on the bench. Trey was an excellent goaltender, but he always started off the preseason slowly, and his teammates just weren't supporting him enough defensively. Brad was almost certain that Reynolds had arranged it so that the better players shot against the better goalie, Trey, and the weaker ones against Sage, a potentially skilled but inexperienced sophomore. Brad felt bad that he and T. J. were getting so many past his old buddy, but he couldn't help it. Playing on a line with T. J. was like playing on a line with Wayne Gretzky. Goalies were a mere triviality. They hadn't played together in so long that Brad had almost forgotten that feeling.

"Not too shabby, guys," Reynolds praised the three linemates as they skated over to the bench for a line change. Then he barked at Team B, "B, let's see some defense out there! Back-check, give your goalie some protection." He let them play for another couple of minutes, and then blew on his whistle. "All right, that's enough for today. Tomorrow Ryan'll work with the goaltenders and the rest

53

of you will work on your defense, and that goes for Team B especially. The key to this game is checking, boys. I'm not saying you have to be gorillas on ice, but you don't just let the other team walk all over you either. So tomorrow morning we'll meet out on the track at six-thirty sharp. Any questions?"

"Yeah, are you always this big a slave driver?" Brett asked.

"Yes," Reynolds replied dryly. "Any other questions? Okay, go hit the showers."

As the teammates began to traipse into the locker room in twos and threes, Brad noticed Trey was looking uncharacteristically glum. "Hey, what's up?" he asked as they entered the locker room.

Shrugging, Trey sat down on the bench and began removing his goalie pads. Somebody had turned on the radio in the adjoining weight room, so the room was pulsing with rock music.

"Trey, it's only the first practice," Brad said in exasperation. "Reynolds knows how good you are."

"No kidding, but, God, Brad, I let in six goals. Six goals!"

"Trey, it was only one scrimmage. Don't get so down on yourself."

"Yeah, you should talk. You and T. J. were doing great."

Brad's eyes flickered, and not responding, he spun the dial on his dented gray locker.

"It must be great playing with T. J.," Trey said. "You're finally on a line with someone who can keep up with you."

Brad thrust open his locker. "Yeah, great."

"What's the matter?" Trey asked.

"It's just hard," Brad said. "I can't let him do better than me. Every time he scores, I feel I have to."

"Don't worry about what he's doing," Trey said. "Just concentrate on yourself."

"I can't help it, Trey, we're really competitive. He's just waiting to get one up on me."

"Brad, he's just trying to earn a spot on the team," Trey said. "Give him a chance. He's your brother."

Brad shook his head. "Forget it, you don't understand," he said.

Shaking his head, Trey peeled off his jersey.

Brad hurriedly showered and got changed, and then returned back out to the arena. He was hunting around for a ride home, when a voice shouted, "Brad! Hey, Brad!" As Brad glanced up, Jessica came rushing down from the bleachers. "Hey, Jess," he said.

"Brad, have you seen Trey?"

"Yeah, he's still in the locker room."

"Is he pretty upset?" Jessica asked.

"Yeah, I tried to talk to him, but he wouldn't listen."

"I guess I'll give it a try," Jessica said. "By the way, you were phenomenal out there."

"Thanks. So what are you doing here?"

"The yearbook meeting let out early so I thought I'd pop over and see how things were doing. So how did you like playing on a line with your brother? You guys really clicked out there."

"Look, Jessica, just give me a break about T. J.,

all right? I'm sick of everybody asking me about him."

Jessica stared at him. "Sorry. I'm going to go wait for Trey."

As she left, Brad sighed and ran a hand through his blond hair.

"Yo, McKendrick, you need a ride home?" Russ called from the stands.

"Yeah, thanks," Brad yelled back.

Russ laughed. "I was talking to your brother, lamebrain," he said, coming down the steps. "But I guess you can have one."

"Forget it, I'll get a ride from someone else," Brad said coolly.

"Brad, I was just kidding," Russ said. "Hey, T. J., hurry up."

"All right, all right. I'm coming!" T. J. shouted.

Brad glanced in the direction of his brother's voice, finally locating him talking with a girl by the exit. His face darkened as he realized who the girl was. Sherry.

"Okay, I'll see you then, T. J.," Sherry was saying as Brad got close enough to hear.

"Okay, see you, Sherry."

As she disappeared out the exit, T. J. said, "Brad, you're not going to believe what that jerk McCann just said to me. He—"

"Come on, Russ is waiting," Brad cut in shortly. As his brother stared after him bewildered, Brad pulled open the heavy orange door and slammed out.

# CHAPTER SEVEN

BRUSHING A DAMP shirt sleeve across his glistening forehead, T. J. grabbed his bottle of Gatorade and sank heavily onto the bench. It was the fifth day of practice, and T. J. had never been so exhausted in his life.

Today, Reynolds had been working them primarily in skating—skating backward, skating with one leg, skating in a square—and game situation drills—single leg stops, pivoting, turn gliding. It was sheer misery. As T. J. watched some of his teammates perform a five-on-three defensive face-off drill, he tried to remember what he had for homework that night. It was a lot—an honors English paper to write, two tests to study for, and a lab report to complete. In addition, he had promised to meet Sherry at the library to help her with her algebra homework.

T. J. wished he had never agreed to tutor Sherry in math. He had nothing against her—she was a nice girl and a good friend, the first friend he'd made at Bayview on his own without Brad—but between practice and school he was lucky he had time to finish his own homework, never mind help Sherry with hers.

"Come on, Ames," Reynolds barked, "Stay with him. I don't care if you have to stick to him like glue, you stay with him until that puck is out of your zone." A moment later, he shook his head and ordered, "Brett, go in for Ames." As Cory Ames nervously skated over to him, the coach said, "Cory, don't fore-check so fast—you're trying to let speed compensate for precision. Slow down a little and you'll be able to fake a check to make the puck carrier commit himself. Ryan!" he yelled. "Take this kid down to the other end of the ice and show him how to fore-check!" He turned back to Cory. "Other than that, kid, you're doing fine out there. It's better to iron it out now than in a game, right?"

T. J. smiled. In his own blustery way, Reynolds was trying to tell the gawky freshman to relax, and that he had made the team. While Reynolds appeared cool and crisp on the outside and was always blowing off steam, he never let a kid get discouraged or lose confidence, and T. J. liked that.

"Hey, T. J.," Steve said. He and Brad sat on the bench next to him. "Good practice."

"Thanks."

"Yeah, T. J., you did great. I wish I was as good as you are," Greg Winslow said from beside him. Greg was a fourteen-year-old freshman forward who for some reason had latched onto T. J. as a role model. He was a nice kid and a potentially good hockey player, but the way he hero-worshipped him and hung on his every word reminded T. J. of Jory.

His face hard, Brad slid further down the bench.

"Hey, do you need a ride home? My mom can give you one."

T. J. bit back a grin. "I would, but since practice didn't start till three today, I went home and got my car. Too bad your mom's coming. I would've given you a ride."

Greg pounced on that like a cat on a mouse. "Well, I can call her, maybe," he said.

"Yeah, but she's probably already on her way."

Greg's face fell. "Oh, yeah."

T. J. suppressed another grin, and tried to remember if he had ever worshipped an older teammate like this. "Hey, maybe next time."

The words worked like magic, and Greg brightened. "Okay," he said. "Thanks, T. J."

Shaking his head, Brad stared into space.

Coach Reynolds suddenly shrilled on his whistle. "All right, come on over here. I've got a couple of announcements to make."

As the team spilled onto the bench in their blue and white practice jerseys, Reynolds said, "Okay, I suppose some of you are interested in who I chose for the final cut. Well, I've decided to keep everybody. Now obviously that means that some of you younger, more inexperienced kids aren't going to get a whole heck of a lot of playing time, but that's why I'm keeping you—so you'll gain experience. You'll learn more every practice you come to, every game you watch, and even if it's only for a few minutes, I promise—you will play.

"Now for the rest of you, I'm looking at a starting lineup that will be like this: first line, Steve, T. J., and Brad; second line, Mike, Glen, and Tony; third line, Brett, Ron, and Matt; and fourth line, Cory, Will, and Greg. For defensemen, it will be Russ and Mark, Max and Bobby, and Danny and Kirk, in that order. Trey will be our first goalie and Sage our second. There may be some changes made later on, but for now that's the way we're going to keep things. Okay, now after much consideration, I've decided that your cocaptains are going to be Brad and T. J., whom I'll talk to after practice."

T. J.'s eyes widened in shock. Brad he had expected, but himself? At a new school?

"Are there any questions?" Reynolds asked, glancing around. "Okay, congratulations to you all, and have a good day. You deserve it."

Instantly T. J. and Brad were surrounded by their teammates, "Congratulations!" Trey said, slapping them both on the back. "See, man, I told you you'd get it," he told Brad.

As his friends gave him high fives and patted him on the shoulder, Brad tried to smile. But as he looked at T. J., his eyes narrowed, and his hands clenched inside his gloves.

"You two should be very proud of yourselves," Reynolds told T. J. and Brad a few moments later. "I don't think I've ever appointed two nonseniors as cocaptains. To be honest with you, I think that you guys would be better off playing in a junior league somewhere, or at a really good prep school, but you're not, so I'm just glad to have you on my team. I assume the two of you are planning to play in college, or maybe even try to go pro?" They both nodded. "Well, still, this team is a very good stepping-stone. I know we can take the league title this year, and I'm also confident that we can make it far in the state tourney. I'm going to be expecting a lot of leadership out of you guys this season, and may even have you take over the warm-ups and some of the drills, so that Coach Ryan and I can give some of the other players individual attention in their weaknesses. So good luck and congratulations." He shook hands with both of them, and then disappeared into the locker room.

T. J. glanced at Brad, unsure of what to say. His brother didn't exactly look thrilled. But before he could say anything, Brad said abruptly, "Look, I'm gonna get a ride home with Steve," and skated off.

A few minutes later, T. J. was heading for his car when Steve's Datsun suddenly pulled up beside him. In front were Steve and Brad, and in back, Trey, Mark, and Brett. Brad was staring straight ahead. "Hey, if it isn't Captain T. J.," Trey commented, hanging out the window. "Tell me, T. J.," he said in a deep, Walter Cronkite voice. "Does this token of leadership feel long overdue?" He held a pretend microphone in front of T. J.'s face.

T. J. burst out laughing. "Trey, you are such a geek."

"Yep, that's what people call me," Trey agreed. "Well, just wanted to say congrats. Later, T. J." As they squealed off, T. J. grinned. But his grin faded as he thought of Brad. It wasn't hard to tell he was furious. Shaking his head, T. J. slid behind the wheel, wondering what it would be like when they saw each other at home.

"T. J.! Brad told us the good news," Barbara McKendrick exclaimed excitedly, coming around the kitchen table and kissing her son's cheek. "I'm so happy for you."

"Thanks, Mom. Hey, you wouldn't have by any chance saved me any supper, would you?" T. J. asked.

His mother smiled. "No, I'm just going to let one of my firstborn sons starve to death," she said, opening the refrigerator and drawing out a plastic-wrapped plate of spaghetti.

"Good, because I've never been so hungry in my life," T. J. said.

"Oh, I'm sure. So how was school today?" his mother asked as she removed the plastic and stuck the plate into the microwave. "Any better?"

"Yeah, it wasn't bad, actually," T. J. told her, leaning his hockey stick against the wall and sliding into a chair. "I'm really starting to make some friends, especially with the guys on the hockey team." He grinned. "There's this one little kid, who I swear must think I'm Wayne Gretzky or something. He follows me around like a puppy."

Barbara McKendrick laughed. "But that's so sweet," she said, sitting down opposite him. "You should be flattered."

"Hey, I hear you got made cocaptain," Chris commented, swaggering into the room.

"Yep."

Chris grinned. "It looks like I'm gonna be giving you guys some competition next year. I made captain of my team too."

"Yeah? Awesome. You sound a little cocky though, don't you?" T. J. asked.

"Not cocky. Confident. Better watch out for first line center, Teej," he said.

"Yeah, I'll say that's confident. Mom, want to get this kid a muzzle?"

"Gladly," Mrs. McKendrick said, laughing.

"Mom, Mom, guess what? I just beat Brad at Trivial Pursuit," Jory exclaimed, bursting into the room with Brad following.

Chris arched an eyebrow. "He beat *you* at Trivial Pursuit?" he asked Brad.

"Hey, it was the stupid Disney edition, okay?" Brad defended himself.

"Come on, come see the question I beat him on," Jory urged.

"Okay, okay we're coming," his mother said.

As Mrs. McKendrick and Chris followed Jory into the living room, Brad and T. J. stared at each other. Finally, T. J. said, "Look, Brad, you've been ticked at me since practice. You're mad that I got made cocaptain aren't you? Come on, Brad," T. J. said when Brad didn't respond. "I've got just as much right to it as you do."

Brad scoffed. "Hardly, T. J. I've been slaving on that team since I was a freshman."

"So? It's not like I've never played the game before," T. J. said shortly.

"It doesn't matter! I've been playing for Bayview for three years and you haven't even played one game for them!"

"Look, Brad, it's not my fault that I got yanked

**63**

out of Hayden! I didn't ask to go to Bayview. You think I wanted to leave all my friends and go to a new school? It's hard enough going there without you acting like such a jerk."

"You're the one who's acting like a jerk, T. J."

"You're just afraid that I'm going to do better than you, and you can't take it!"

"Are you kidding? You may be Dad's precious genius, but you're never going to be better than me at hockey. And if you think I'm playing on a line with you, you're crazy. So let's just see who Reynolds sends down a line, T. J.," Brad challenged his brother.

"Yeah, well have fun playing with McCann," T. J. snapped.

Brad shoved his brother into the refrigerator, and T. J. promptly pushed him back. They were grappling with each other when their father strode into the room and ripped them apart.

"What on earth is going on in here?" Mr. McKendrick demanded, his face red.

"Nothing," Brad said.

"Nothing?" Mr. McKendrick asked.

"Nothing other than the fact that T. J. is an obnoxious jerk."

"Hey, you're the one who's threatening to quit the line," T. J. said.

"I'm not threatening to quit the line. I'm threatening to get you kicked off it," Brad said.

T. J.'s green eyes flashed. "Fat chance!"

"Look, I don't know what this is about," their father began, "but you two have an obligation to your teammates. You can't just go back on that because of personal differences."

"He started it," T. J. said.

"I don't care who started it, Thomas, I just want it stopped."

Suddenly the telephone rang, and to T. J.'s relief after the third ring Chris called out, "Yo, T. J., telephone."

His father sighed. "Don't stay on too long," he said. "I imagine you've got quite a bit of homework to do."

"Right, Dad." Happy to get out of the room, T. J. grabbed his books and escaped into the living room.

"Here. I think it's Kevin," Chris told him, handing his brother the cordless. He was down on the floor, playing Trivial Pursuit with his mother and Jory and sneaking glances at *Three's Company*.

"Is everything okay in there, T. J.?" his mother asked.

Nodding, T. J. carried the phone up to his room and flopped down onto the bed. "Hello?" he said, switching on the stereo.

"Hey, Teej, it's Kevin."

"And Tricia on the kitchen extension," Tricia added.

"Hi. How're you guys doing?"

"Pretty good," Kevin replied.

"How's hockey going?"

"The team looks good. Did you hear who got made captain?"

"No, who?"

"Anderson."

"That jerk?"

"No kidding," Kevin said.

**65**

"Better not get him worked up about it, T. J.," Tricia warned, "or, believe me, you'll never get him off the subject. He's been complaining about this for two days."

"Well, it's just because he's a senior, Trish. If you were still at Hayden, Teej, it wouldn't have happened. So who got captain at Bayview?"

T. J. sighed. "My brother and I."

"T. J., that's wonderful," Tricia said. "Congratulations. You don't sound too happy about it, though."

"It's just my brother. He's being a real jerk about it."

"I guess it must be tough for him," Tricia said. "He probably was counting on being captain, just like you were at Hayden."

"Well, I didn't ask to switch schools. Whose side are you on, anyway?"

"I'm not on anyone's side, T. J. I'm just saying that Brad's probably just as upset about you being at Bayview as you are. Maybe the two of you should talk about how you feel."

"Yeah, well it's not easy to talk to someone who's barely speaking to you."

"Hey, let's get off this subject," Kevin cut in. "Other than hockey, how's Bayview?"

"Okay." T. J. suddenly realized he didn't want to talk to Kevin and Tricia anymore. How could they understand how he felt? They were still at Hayden, with all their friends—where he should be. He gave short answers to a few more questions from Kevin, then found an excuse to hang up.

Sighing, he returned to his homework. Talking

to his friends should have made him feel better. Instead, he felt worse than ever.

It was the first game of the season, and the Bayview Jets were playing against the Brentwood Hawks. They were in the Brentwood arena and the stands were packed. T. J. went to take the opening face-off, his stomach in knots. Brad and Steve were to his right and left, Russ and Mark in back, and Trey in goal.

As the referee, in his black and white striped shirt, bent over the face-off circle at center ice, T. J. swallowed hard. The referee held the puck over his right shoulder and motioned both centers back a bit from the face-off spot. T. J. and the Hawks' center stared down at the spot, their sticks poised a few inches off the ice as they anticipated the drop. The referee dropped the puck and the two centers slashed their sticks at it. T. J. won the draw, sliding the disk back to Brad, who sent it into the Hawks' zone and took off after it. Brad caught it on his stick again, and that was the last T. J. saw of the puck.

Midway through the first period, Brad overtook a Brentwood defenseman trying to carry the puck out of his defensive zone. Placing his stick under the defenseman's he lifted it off the ice. He then scooped the puck back toward him with his own stick and headed toward the goal.

The move caught the Hawks' players going the other way, leaving only one defenseman back. T. J. reversed his direction, and it was a two on one. Brad, skating down the right lane, was shifting the puck back and forth against his stick's blade. T. J.

was riding in on the goalkeeper in the left lane, and the lone defenseman was trying to stay in the middle of the two forwards. Come on, Brad, pass it, T. J. thought. He was right in front of the crease and had an open shot over the goaltender's right shoulder. But instead of passing, Brad went for the shot himself, only to have the goalie catch it easily in his large mitt. Sighing, T. J. rapped his stick onto the ice.

"Brad, what were you doing? I was right open!" T. J. said a few minutes later as they skated over to the bench for a line change.

Not even looking at him, Brad climbed over the boards and took a drink out of his water bottle.

"Come on, will you pass the puck?" When Brad didn't respond, T. J. sank down onto the bench in frustration.

By the end of the first period, T. J. had had the puck only three times, and only because he had won it on a face-off or had intercepted it from an opposing player. Even Steve, their linemate, hadn't had much control over it. By some miracle, Brentwood hadn't yet scored on them, and the game was 0–0.

"What the hell do you think you're doing?" T. J. demanded of Brad as the team filed into the locker room. "You're costing us the game!"

"Get out of my face," Brad said, setting his stick against a locker.

T. J. threw his helmet onto the floor. "Are you blind? I was open four times! We could have been up 4–0!"

"Don't flatter yourself, T. J.," Brad replied.

"Look, I'm just telling you that you'd better pass the puck," T. J. snapped.

"Or what?" Brad asked.

"Hey, guys, come on," Trey, who had come up behind them, said in a low voice. "Calm down."

"Stay out of my way, T. J.," Brad told his brother. He elbowed past him and sat down on the bench.

After Reynolds had harped about how they needed to come together and play as a team, the Jets streamed back out onto the ice. As T. J. got set for the draw, he glanced over at his brother, who was staring stormily ahead. Sighing, he returned his gaze to the face-off circle.

T. J. got the puck from the face-off, and once he had it, he refused to give it up. Pushing the puck forward with the blade of his stick, he headed up the ice. At the Hawks' blue line, he was blocked trying to slip through the defense. Shooting the rubber into the backboards, he darted past two green and white shirted defensemen and raced after it.

A Brentwood defenseman jabbed his shoulder into T. J.'s side, and T. J. could feel his stick rattling against the boards as they went after the loose puck.

Finally digging the disk out of the corner, T. J. swung around the boards. Brad was in front of the net, but T. J. wasn't about to relinquish the puck. Even though a defenseman was on his tail, T. J. tried to get into a good position himself.

Suddenly the defenseman cut in front of him and hooked the puck off T. J.'s stick. Rushing down the length of the ice, he passed it to a forward, who curled it over Trey's right shoulder. 1–0 Hawks.

"Yeah, you're really doing great, T. J.," Brad said, skating past him.

T. J. gritted his teeth and refused to pass once to Brad during the rest of the period. During the few times that Brad had control of the puck, he continued keeping it away from T. J.

When the team returned back to the locker room, Coach Reynolds pulled the brothers aside. "What is the matter with you two? What do you think this is, a competition?"

They both shuffled uncomfortably. "This is not an individual sport, this is a team sport, and the object is to play as a team," he said. "You two are supposed to be linemates, but you've barely passed to each other all night, and on top of that, you're both making ridiculous shots. You're the cocaptains; you're supposed to set an example. And since you're not setting one, I'm going to make you an example. I'm benching both of you for the third period."

"I've never been benched in my life!" Brad said.

"Well then, I guess that means you've never played a game as terribly as this in your life," Reynolds replied.

"Coach, come on!" Brad said.

"Look, just put me on another line," T. J. said.

"No," Reynolds said. "You play on the original line or you don't play on any line. Now you're both benched and that's it."

"Thanks a lot, Brad," T. J. said as Reynolds strode away.

"Hey, don't blame me," Brad responded.

A while later, as the clock began ticking away the minutes in the third period, T. J. folded his arms across his chest and leaned back against the glass partition separating him from the crowd.

The score remained 1–0 until, with five minutes left in the game, the Hawks' defenseman who had stolen the puck from T. J. faked toward the net and then flicked a wrist shot over Trey's left shoulder. As the player's stick lifted in victory, T. J. stood up. "Coach, come on, put me in," he said. "There's only five minutes left."

"Sit down, McKendrick," Reynolds ordered. "Ron, go in for Glen."

Fuming, T. J. sank back onto the bench. "I can't believe he's not putting you in," Greg said from beside him.

T. J. just stared ahead, his face expressionless.

Steve got two more shots on goal and Ron one, but all were fruitless. Bayview wound up losing 2–0.

"A terrible effort," Reynolds said once the game was over and the players were in the locker room. Everyone was quiet. "I want to see some serious changes out there, both in strategy and in the attitudes of certain players." He froze Brad and T. J. with a hard look. "We're playing Crestwood in two days, and I expect a complete turnaround by then. Now go get ready for the ride home."

Glaring at Brad, T. J. bent down and began unlacing his skates.

# CHAPTER EIGHT

THAT NIGHT ON the way back to Bayview, Brad stared out the bus window, the darkness lit only by the wink of an occasional streetlight. The night was cold, and flakes of snow were dusting the window. A Hammer song came on the radio, and someone in back yelled for the bus driver to turn the sound up.

"You okay?" Trey asked from beside him.

Nodding, Brad shifted his gaze to the back of the torn, green vinyl seat in front of him.

"Brad, you've got to learn to play with him," Trey said. "I've seen you, you guys, you could be awesome together."

Brad shook his head. "I can't believe I got benched," he said.

"You deserved it, man. You should have seen some of the shots you were taking," Trey told him.

"Thanks," Brad said.

"Look, you know what I mean," Trey said. "I'm not saying I was playing great tonight either, but at least I tried. You were playing like T. J. was on the other team. Then you got him so that he wasn't passing, because he knew that if he did, he'd never get the puck back again."

"So it's all my fault?" Brad asked.

"Look, Brad, I'm your best friend. I'm just trying to make you take a look at what you're doing to yourself. And it's not even just to yourself. It's to the whole team."

"You should have heard the speech Reynolds gave us," Brad said. "He totally bawled us out. I can't afford any more games like this."

"Then don't. You don't have to like playing with him, Brad," Trey said. "You just have to play with him."

Sighing, Brad returned his gaze back out the window.

Once they arrived at Bayview High, Brad climbed down the bus steps, his stick in one hand and his duffel bag in the other. The air was crisp and the sky dark. "Brad, you getting a ride home with us?" Trey asked behind him. He, Steve, and Greg were driving home with T. J.

"With him? Get real," Brad replied, going over to Russ's car.

Twenty minutes later, when his friend pulled up in front of his house, Brad saw that T. J.'s car wasn't back yet. T. J. had probably stopped for pizza—with *Brad's* friends. He slammed the car door with more force than was really necessary.

When Brad entered the living room, he found his mother sitting on the couch, with the TV on, reading a Danielle Steel novel. "Hi, honey," she said, looking up from her book. "How was the game?"

Brad shrugged.

**73**

"Did you win?"

Brad took off his letter jacket. "No, we lost, two—zero."

"Oh, that's too bad," Mrs. McKendrick said. "Well, it's only the first game. How'd you do?"

Brad sighed.

"Well, don't worry about it, you've got a whole season left," she said.

"I guess."

His mother glanced at him and then said, "You look tired. Why don't you go up to bed."

Nodding, Brad headed up the stairs. He met Chris going down the hallway to his room. "Hey, did you win?" Chris asked.

Brad opened the door to his bedroom. "No, we didn't win."

"Well, did you score?"

"Look, Chris, just leave me alone."

Chris stared at him. "Sorry," he said.

Stepping into his room, Brad set his duffel bag and stick on the floor, and then closed the door behind him. He wanted to be in bed, at least pretending to be asleep, before T. J. got home.


Brad skimmed around the ice of the Bayview High arena, so pumped up he could hardly think. Although it was only the pregame skate, he performed it briskly and speedily, unlike his teammates, who looked as if they were on their way to a funeral. Brad's butterflies were fluttering around in the form of energy and hyperactivity, and he had to skate swiftly in order to keep himself occupied. The Bayview Jets were circling one half of the rink and the Crestwood Eagles the other. As he skated past T. J. they both looked the other way, and Brad quickly glanced up into the crowd.

The stands were beginning to fill up, with people trickling in steadily. It was quite an impressive crowd for a high school hockey team's first home game of the season, mostly teachers, students, and the players' excited families. As he expected Brad was able to pick out his own family sitting a couple of rows up from the penalty box. Chris had this thing about ragging on the opposing team's penalty servers. As Jory noticed his older brother looking up at them, he smiled and began waving eagerly, and despite himself Brad grinned and waved back.

"You know, McKendrick, your brother's a real jerk. I hope that you don't turn out to be as cocky as he is."

Brad whirled around angrily, to see Glen McCann with his face a couple of inches from T. J.'s. "McCann, if you want to see a real jerk take a look in the mirror," T. J. replied coolly. "And keep your mouth shut about my brother."

As the teams began to stream off the ice and into the locker room, Brad stole a glance at his brother, his anger at Glen giving way to more confusing emotions.

"Come on, come on, everybody sit down," Coach Ryan said anxiously, tugging on his hair. There was a nervous tic in his left eye, and his arms were flailing up and down like a nervous scarecrow's. "Everybody take a seat."

Calmer, Reynolds said evenly, "Okay, guys, you know the game plan. T. J.'s line out first, and Russ and Mark on defense. Now, I know that after the loss the other night you're all nervous, but just take it easy out there, okay? We should be able to take these guys. From what I've heard from some of the other coaches, their defense is full of holes, so there ought to be no problem penetrating it. Play aggressively and body check, and you should be able to put a lid on their offense. And play as a team. I don't want to see any showboating out there, especially from people who should be setting an example. You know you're the better team, and Ryan and I know you're the better team, but now you've got to prove that to Crestwood. So go out there and show them who's boss, and you'll skate away with your first victory."

"Can I add something, coach?" Brad asked.

"Sure, I'm glad someone seems to be alive here."

Brad raised his fist. "Let's go make some eagles extinct!"

Smiling, Reynolds said, "I couldn't agree more."

The referee motioned both centers back an inch from the face-off circle and then carefully dropped the puck between them. Both T. J. and the Crestwood center slapped their sticks at it, with T. J. winning the draw and flipping the puck back to Brad.

Catching the frozen rubber disk on the end of his blade, Brad skated across the Crestwood blue line, spraying a stream of silver ice chips into the air as he swerved around an opposing defenseman. He moved in closer to the net and then faked to the right, pulling the Crestwood goalie to one side.

Instantly, Brad drew his stick back and slammed the rubber into the opposite corner of the cage. Almost simultaneously he was swarmed by a mob of his teammates.

Within ten minutes, the score was Bayview 3 and Crestwood 0, with Brad having scored two goals, Steve one, and T. J. three assists. In the nets, Trey was outstanding, deflecting pucks the way Superman deflected bullets, and the rest of the team, having found the holes in Crestwood's Swiss-cheese defense, was playing phenomenally as well. The crowd was going wild, and if there was one thing that got Brad psyched it was an enthusiastic crowd. He could actually feel the adrenaline pumping.

Midway through the second period, T. J. completed a fantastic breakaway play. Stopping, he passed the puck back to Brad. Brad hesitated a moment, memories of T. J.'s defense of him to Glen and of the coach's warning clashing in his brain with all his anger and resentment of T. J. Then he slid the puck back to his brother. T. J. drove the puck over the goaltender's right shoulder and into the net, with the goalie never moving. As the thick cord mesh sagged and the red light popped on, T. J.'s stick flew up in victory. It was his first goal as a Bayview Jet.

As his teammates began to congregate around his brother, Brad skated over to the Crestwood's goaltender, whom he knew from hockey camp. "Hey, Jason, can I have that puck?" he asked in a low voice.

Jason nodded, and fished it out of the net with his stick. "Yeah, sure. Hey, Brad, tell me something. Is it me or am I being provided with no defense?"

"You're being provided with no defense," Brad said immediately.

Jason exhaled in relief, and straightened his face mask. "Good. I thought I was losing it there for a while."

Brad slapped his friend's shoulder. "You are losing it, Jase," he said cheerfully. Then he grinned and added as he skated away, "Hey, break a leg, okay?"

"Hey, Brad," Jason called back to him. "Hockey mask, Jason, Friday the thirteenth—think about it."

"You goalies, you take everything so seriously."

"I certainly hope you were paying that goalie off," Steve remarked as Brad plopped next to him on the bench.

Brad just smiled, and stashed the puck behind his water bottle.

Bayview ended up with a shutout, a lopsided score of 9–0. "For a well-played game, I'm treating everyone to a pizza at Misty's," Reynolds announced in the locker room afterward. As the team began cheering, he held up his hand and said, "But I want you to know that it's not just because you won, it's because you exhibited good teamwork and worked as a unit."

"A hat trick, huh, McKendrick?" Trey commented a few minutes later, as he sat down next to Brad and began removing his thick goaltender's gloves. "Not bad, not bad. And twin brother over there with two goals. You and he going for a record or something? The first twins in Bayview High history to win twin MVP trophies?"

"Don't push it, Trey," Brad responded shortly. "I'm just doing what I have to."

Fifteen minutes later, as Brad opened the locker room door and stepped out into the frigid, dimly lit parking lot, he was immediately encircled by his mother, father, and two younger brothers. "Brad, congratulations. I'm so proud of you," his mother squealed, squeezing his shoulder.

"Nice game son," his father said with a pleased smile on his face.

"You know that guy that slashed you in the third period—Robertson?" Chris asked excitedly. "Well, you should have heard what I said to him while he was in the penalty box. I thought he was gonna come up into the stands and rip my head off!"

"Well, it would serve you right, Christopher," his mother chided him. "Where on earth did you pick up such a habit?"

As Chris glanced at Brad, Mrs. McKendrick rolled her eyes. "I should have known," she said. "I just hope Jory doesn't pick it up."

Jory just shivered and began shuffling around to keep warm.

"Hey, guys," T. J. said, strolling over to them. Behind him were Trey, Russ, Steve, and Greg.

"T. J., hi," his mother said brightly. "You played so well tonight. All of you did," she added, looking at her son's four teammates.

"Not me, I didn't even play," Greg said glumly. Trey turned around and glanced at him, apparently just noticing him for the first time.

"Can you guys take my stuff home?" T. J. asked, nodding at his duffel bag and hockey stick.

"Sure," his mother said, reaching out for them. "Coach Reynolds is taking you all to Misty's?"

"Yeah, did you talk to him?" Brad asked. Great, he thought.

"Yes, he came up to us during the second intermission. He told us how well you two were doing, and how you, T. J., and Steve all play so wonderfully together." Brad raised an eyebrow. "That was very nice of him, don't you think?"

"Did he say anything about me, Mrs. M.?" Trey asked.

"Sorry, Trey," Mrs. McKendrick replied.

"Well, we should probably get going," T. J. commented, as a carload of their teammates whipped past them, honking.

"Well, not too late, huh, guys?" Mr. McKendrick said.

Brad nodded. "Hey, Chris, take my stuff home, all right?" he asked, his breath spiraling out in cold wisps.

Chris glared at him, and then reluctantly unstuffed his hands from his pockets. "Why don't you do it yourself?" he demanded.

"Why should I? I've got you." Winking at him, he said good-bye to his parents, and then followed his friends and T. J. to Steve's car.

"Well, see you later, guys," Steve said, stopping the car in front of the McKendricks' house later that night. "Awesome game tonight."

"Yeah, you too, man," Brad said as he opened the car door.

"See you tomorrow, Stevo," T. J. said, giving his friend a high five. "Nice playing."

As Steve pulled away from the curb, T. J. headed toward the house.

Brad hesitated, and then said quietly, "T. J., wait a minute."

His brother sighed and turned around. "What?"

Slowly, Brad reached into his jacket pocket and drew out the puck that Jason had given him. "Here," he said, extending it. "It's from your first goal . . . it's for luck."

His eyes never leaving the puck, T. J. slowly accepted it, flipping it and reflipping it in his hand. Finally he lifted up his head. "Thanks," he said.

"The reason I asked you here, Brad," Mr. Wood began, pressing his elbows to his desk, "is that as a high school junior, it is time to start thinking about your college plans and your goals for the future. Now do you have any idea of what college you would like to attend?"

"I'm not sure," Brad told his guidance counselor uncomfortably. "I guess I've been kind of considering BC and BU."

"Any particular reason you're considering them?"

"Well, mostly because they both have good hockey programs."

Mr. Wood gazed at him for a moment, his hands cupping his chin. Finally, he said, "Hockey is fine, Brad, but what about academics? What are you interested in majoring in?"

"I don't know, maybe journalism or something," Brad responded.

"Then you're interested in writing?"

"Yeah, I want to try to become a professional hockey player and maybe write on the side."

The guidance counselor sighed. "Brad, those are two pretty lofty ambitions, but I'm afraid that the odds of achieving them aren't very good. If you're interested in writing, why don't you plan to go into something like public relations, rather than counting on making it in pro hockey."

When Brad didn't reply, Mr. Wood said, "Brad you have to admit that both your goals are rather unrealistic."

"Hey, my own coach thinks I could go pro," Brad said. "You don't know anything about it."

"Nevertheless, Brad, even for a talented player like you, becoming a professional athlete is a long shot. You need an alternative goal if that doesn't pan out," Mr. Wood responded.

"Yeah, well look me up in five years," Brad said, standing up, "and then we'll see about that." Picking up his notebook, he pulled open the door and stalked out.

# CHAPTER NINE

T. J. WAS PASSING by the doorway to Brad's room when he saw his brother lying on his bed, staring at the ceiling. He hesitated, and then entered the room. "What's the matter?" he asked as Brad glanced over at him.

"Nothing."

"You sure?"

"I don't know. I got into an argument with my guidance counselor today."

"Over what?" T. J. asked.

"He thought my goals were unrealistic," Brad responded.

"Why? What are they?"

"To be a hockey player and a writer."

T. J. sat down on the edge of Brad's bed. "And your guidance counselor told you to not even bother?"

"Yeah."

"That sounds like what my guidance counselor at Hayden said when I told her that I wanted to go pro."

Brad glanced at him. "You?"

T. J. nodded.

**83**

"But I thought you wanted to be a lawyer," Brad said.

T. J. stood up. "No, Dad wants me to be a lawyer."

"I thought you did too."

T. J. scoffed. "No way."

"Well, then why don't you tell Dad?" Brad asked.

"I've tried; he doesn't listen," T. J. replied. "Now if you told him you wanted to be a hockey player, he'd probably think it was great, but when I told him, I got yelled at."

"What's that supposed to mean?"

"Come on, Brad, he supports you in everything you do."

"Me? You're the one he thinks is perfect," Brad said.

"Brad, he never thinks anything I do is good enough," T. J. replied.

They were silent a moment, both gazing at the wall. Then T. J. said, "I didn't know you liked to write."

Brad nodded.

"What about?"

"Different things."

"I can't picture you writing."

Brad shrugged. "Look, I've got to do my algebra homework."

Nodding, T. J. opened the door.

As T. J. was studying for his English test that night, sharp voices suddenly rose from downstairs. Shaking his head, he turned up his television, tuned to a Bruins/Red Wings game. It seemed he was turning up the TV to drown out his parents' angry voices more and more.

A couple of minutes later, Brad strode in, letting the door slam behind him. "You know, you'd think that with Chris and Jory home, they could be just a little bit more discreet," he said fiercely, flopping down onto T. J.'s bed.

"Yeah, no kidding," T. J. replied, looking up from his desk. "Maybe we should bring them in here, play a game with them or something."

A light tap suddenly sounded at T. J.'s door, and a moment later, Chris and Jory stepped into the room, Jory red eyed and Chris stony faced.

"Hey, you guys want to play a game or something?" Brad asked.

"Yeah, sure."

"Yeah, let's play Trivial Pursuit."

"No!" Brad and Chris said at the same time.

"How about Monopoly?" T. J. suggested.

"But I never win at that," Jory protested.

Brad and Chris looked at each other. "Perfect," Brad said.

A few minutes later, as T. J. was dealing out the Monopoly money, Chris said, "Hey, you guys have that Christmas tournament in a few days, don't you?"

"Yeah, it starts next Tuesday," T. J. replied.

"What is it, three rounds?"

"Yeah."

"Isn't Hayden in the tournament too?" Chris asked.

Nodding, T. J. rolled the dice.

A half hour later, Brad threw Chris his fourteen-hundred-dollar Boardwalk rent. "I don't get it, every time I pick that stupid guy on a horse I lose," he said.

"But you haven't lost yet," Jory protested.

"Jory, he's got hotels all over the board," Brad replied.

"So?"

"Keep being an optimist, Jor," Brad said, patting his youngest brother's shoulder.

T. J. rose. "I'm going to go get some chips or something," he said. "Anybody want anything?"

"Do you want to butt in if they're still fighting?" Chris asked.

"Just because they're acting like jerks doesn't mean we have to go hungry."

"Well, I guess you can get me some Doritos," Chris said, tossing the dice.

As T. J. stepped out into the hallway, he heard soft, muffled sobbing coming from his parents' bedroom. Sighing, he trudged downstairs.

Their pine-scented Christmas tree stood proudly in the middle of the living room. Strings of lights winked from beneath silver and gold strands of tinsel, casting pastel shadows on the powdery white carpet. Passing the large bay window, T. J. glanced out, and saw only gravel where his father's Cadillac should be.

A few minutes later, arms laden with a bowl of sour-cream-and-onion potato chips and an unopened bag of Doritos, he returned to his room. "Hey, where's Brad and Jory?" he asked, seeing that Chris was alone.

"Jory was starting to fall asleep so Brad's making him go to bed," Chris explained. "So what's going on downstairs?" he asked quietly.

"Nothing, they stopped."

"What are they doing now?" Chris pressed.

"Chris, how should I know? They're just not down there anymore," T. J. said uncomfortably.

Chris eyed him suspiciously for a moment, and then wearily got to his feet. Taking the bag of Doritos, he mumbled, "I've got to go. See you."

A minute after Chris left, Brad returned, quietly closing the door behind him. "Dad gone?" he asked in a low voice.

T. J. nodded. "And Mom's crying."

"Yeah, I heard." Brad hesitated, and then said, "Do you think they're going to split up?"

T. J. stared at him. "I don't know." He paused. "What do you think?"

"Well, this can't go on much longer." They were both quiet for a while. Then Brad said, "I think we should take Chris and Jory out somewhere this weekend. They've both been really upset about Mom and Dad lately."

"I know," T. J. said. "Maybe we can go to a movie or something."

"I know somewhere else really great where we can take them," Brad said, opening the door.

"Where?"

Brad stepped out into the hallway. "This place called Silver Creek."

# CHAPTER TEN

SILVER CREEK WAS just as beautiful and peaceful as Brad remembered. The steep embankment of rocks towered up into the pinkening blue sky, the fleecy white clouds looking like swirls of spun cotton candy. Bony trees that had been bared of their leaves threaded the winding, dusty paths, and lush pines rustled in the dusky breeze. Brad shivered, for a wintry chill pervaded the air, a New England chill that he knew was an almost definite sign of snow.

The last time that Brad had been here had been nearly a year ago, after Bayview had been knocked out of the Division 1 state tournament. Devastated by the loss, and furious with himself for having gone scoreless in the quarterfinals, Brad had thought that Silver Creek seemed like the perfect place to be alone and to sort out his feelings.

Trey had been the one who had first introduced the place to him; it had been the summer before tenth grade, and Brad and Trey had been experimenting with cigarettes. There was always someone home at both their houses, and they were too paranoid to smoke in public, so on the advice of his cousin, Trey had led them here.

Though every once in a while a family or a group of teenagers would come here to hike, for the most part it was secluded, basically because no one seemed to know of its existence. If you walked far enough, you would find a small woodsy area with swings, seesaws, picnic tables, and barbecue fixtures. Beyond the picnic area a grassy hill sloped gently to a thin, silvery creek.

"Brad, can we climb the rocks?" Jory asked eagerly.

Brad smiled. "Yeah, come on," he said, leading the way.

"Are there really caves here?" Chris wanted to know.

"Yeah. I think I'm gonna skip them though. You have to practically crawl in on your hands and knees."

"But we can still go in, right?" Jory asked.

Brad and T. J. exchanged grins. "Right," T. J. said.

This outing really seemed to be doing Chris and Jory some good, Brad thought. First they had gone to the Blackwell Mall, where they had seen the new horror movie *Death Frat*. T. J. had been a little leery about letting Jory see *Death Frat,* but Jory had loved it, and had chattered about it incessantly while they had had ice cream and done Christmas shopping and eaten at McDonald's and all during the car ride to Silver Creek. So far, the day had been a tremendous success.

"Didn't you love the part where the girl ate the

eyeball?" Jory asked, as the brothers began climbing up the rocks. "Wasn't that neat?"

"If this kid turns out to be a mass murderer or something, it's your fault, Brad," T. J. commented.

Brad ignored him. "Yeah, that part was awesome," he agreed.

T. J. shook his head. "Hey, is that little thing a cave? Man, you weren't kidding. Have fun, guys."

As Chris and Jory scurried ahead, Brad and T. J. sat on a rock.

"Don't let me forget to call Sherry tonight," T. J. said, leaning back against the rock. "I was supposed to call her before we left this morning."

Brad jumped down. "I'm not your social secretary," he snapped.

"What's with you?"

"Nothing."

"Come on, Brad, what's your problem?"

Brad just stared into the trees.

"Wait a minute," T. J. said, sitting up. "You don't like Sherry or something, do you?"

Brad didn't respond.

"You do, don't you?" T. J. asked.

Brad whirled on him, "Look, man, it's none of your business, so why don't you just butt out."

"Brad, you don't think I'm interested in her, do you? She's just a friend."

"A pretty good friend," Brad replied.

"Brad, I'm tutoring her in algebra. That's it," T. J. said.

Brad snorted. "Anybody who needs that much tutoring, T. J. . . ."

"Look, Brad, I'll admit that I was interested in her at first. She was the first friend I made at

Bayview. But it just developed into a friendship. If she likes anyone, it's you," T. J. said. "She's always bringing your name up."

"Right, T. J.," Brad said.

"I'm serious, Brad. She asks me questions about you all the time. You should ask her out."

Brad looked at him. "Are you being straight with me?"

"Come on, Brad . . ."

Brad looked at him again, and then slowly broke into a grin, "You'd better be."

T. J. grinned too. "I've never even seen you talking to her," he said.

Brad shook his head. "I don't know what it is. I can never get up the nerve to go over to her."

"Don't worry about it, just get it over with," T. J. said. "She'll be happy."

"Well, maybe."

T. J. hesitated and then said, "Listen . . . I was wondering. Would you let me read something you wrote sometime?"

"Well, I usually don't let anyone read anything I write, but . . . okay," Brad said.

T. J. smiled. "Thanks."

"You guys, we're going into the next cave, all right?" Chris said, crawling out of the underbrush and then straightening up.

"Another one?" T. J. asked skeptically. "A cave's a cave, isn't it?"

"T. J., they're neat. You should try one," Chris replied.

"Sorry, but I've got this thing about being permanently hunched over," T. J. said. "Could be very damaging to my hockey career."

"Well, it's your loss," Chris told him. Shrugging his shoulders, he pushed past Jory and scrambled into the next cave.

"Well, Christopher certainly seems chipper today," Brad commented, raising an eyebrow.

"Yeah, he's been awfully moody lately, have you noticed?"

"Yeah, it's hard not to." Brad lowered his voice. "Don't say anything to Mom and Dad, but about three or four weeks ago, he got into a fight in school and had me forge Dad's signature on the warning he brought home."

T. J.'s jaw dropped. "Are you serious? He did the same thing to me, only I forged Mom's signature."

"What? I thought I got through to him," Brad said.

"Yeah, me too. And he didn't mention anything to me about any previous fight," T. J. said.

"Was the second one about something stupid too?" Brad asked.

"Yeah. This kid said something to him at hockey practice and he blew up," T. J. said.

"He's always had a temper, but not like this," Brad said.

"Do you think we should say anything to him?"

"You'd better believe it. We can't let that little runt get away with this."

As Jory slithered out of the second cave and started up some more rocks, Brad grabbed Chris, who had been about to head after him. "Christopher, T. J. and I were just having a rather interesting conversation about you," Brad said. "It seems you've been holding out on us."

"What do you mean?" Chris asked.

"I mean your little misunderstandings at hockey practice and recess."

Chris looked down. "Oh," he said.

Brad rolled his eyes. " 'Oh,' he says. Chris, what is going on with you? I mean, you promised me you wouldn't get into any more fights."

"Brad, I couldn't help it. This thing came up and—"

"Chris, the 'thing' that came up hardly called for a fistfight," T. J. broke in.

"But you said you understood—both of you did," Chris objected.

"Yeah, but that was when we thought it was a one-time thing," Brad snapped. "We didn't know it was your latest hobby."

"Chris, you can't just beat somebody up every time you disagree with him," T. J. said.

"But it's not every time—it was only twice," Chris argued.

"Well, twice in two weeks is enough, all right?"

Chris sighed. "Look, it won't happen again, okay? I promise."

"You promise? Yeah, that really means a lot now, Chris," Brad scoffed.

"Since when did you get to be such a goody two-shoes?" Chris demanded. "You've gotten into fights before."

"Look, what is with this attitude you're giving lately?" Brad asked.

"Just leave me alone," Chris said.

"Chris, this isn't just about you anymore. If you get into any more fights, the principal'll call in Mom and Dad, and then you'll take Brad and me

**93**

down with you," T. J. said. "Just how many second chances do you think they're going to give you?"

"Well, what do you want me to do? I mean, I already promised I wouldn't get into any more fights. And I haven't in a couple of weeks," Chris added.

"Well, just make sure it stays that way, all right?" T. J. said.

Chris nodded. "All right, So, like, are we done now?" he asked.

"Yeah," Brad said. "We're done."

"Good." Chris took a step toward Jory, who was in the distance hanging around by another cave. Then he turned and asked hesitantly, "Do you think maybe we could come back here again sometime? I've never been someplace I've liked so much."

"Look, I'll make a deal with you," Brad said. "You stay out of trouble, and we'll take you back here in a couple of weeks. Okay?"

Chris nodded, paused as if he were going to say something, and then evidently changed his mind and ran to catch up to Jory.

"Somehow I don't think we got too far," Brad said.

"You got that idea too?" T. J. asked.

"I just hope he stays out of trouble," Brad said, "because with the mood Dad's been in lately . . ."

"Yeah, we'll all get nailed," T. J. finished.

Sobered by this thought, Brad and T. J. followed their younger brothers up the rocks.

# CHAPTER ELEVEN

T. J. SET BRAD'S story on his desk, extremely impressed. He couldn't believe Brad—*Brad*—could write like this. Who would have guessed? He'd written a science fiction story, about a teenager who is terrorized by his evil alter ego. In a way it was kind of ironic, with the writer being a twin. T. J. had been completely engrossed by the story. T. J. was no expert, but he thought it was better than some published stories he'd read. Brad had real talent.

Rising, he went down the hall to Brad's room. His brother was lying on his bed reading a hockey magazine. "Hey," Brad said, his eyes immediately traveling to the folder in T. J.'s hands.

Noticing, T. J. smiled. "I finished your story," he said, sitting down on Brad's bed.

"Yeah?" Brad asked cautiously.

"Yeah. It was good."

Brad's shoulders relaxed.

"You're lucky to have a talent like that."

"So you really liked it?" Brad asked, a smile tugging at his lips.

"It was cool," T. J. replied. "How'd you ever think of something like that?"

Brad shrugged. "I don't know. It just came to me."

"Is all your stuff science fiction?" T. J. asked.

"Some of it," Brad replied. "But I'm into horror the most."

T. J. grinned. "That figures, from the way you watch those slasher movies."

"Yeah. I guess I want to be the next Stephen King," Brad said, grinning also.

"Are you working on anything now?"

"Yeah, another horror," Brad replied. After a pause he went on, "I have some others if you want to read them."

"Yeah, sure," T. J. agreed. "Have you shown them to your English teacher or somebody?"

Brad shook his head. "I don't know. I guess I just don't want them to tell me I'm no good."

"Believe me, that's the last thing they'll tell you," T. J. told him. "You should show somebody."

"I don't know. Maybe," Brad said.

"Mom and Dad don't know about this, do they?"

"No, and don't tell them," Brad replied. "I'll tell them myself someday."

T. J. nodded. "Hey—thanks for letting me read your story," he said.

"No," Brad said. "Thanks for asking to."

"Hey, T. J., Mom and Dad want to see us in the den pronto," Brad said, appearing in T. J.'s doorway.

96

T. J. threw on his denim jacket. "Now? But we've got to get to the rink," he protested, picking up his hockey stick.

"No kidding, so hurry up," Brad replied.

Bayview had soundly knocked off Bennington in the first round of the Christmas tournament, by a lopsided score of 9–1, and the team was now on its way to play the Stoneham Lions. In the Bennington matchup, Brad had scored three goals, Russ one, and T. J. a whopping five, along with three assists. It had reached the point that every time T. J. touched the puck, the Bayview fans would cheer. To T. J.'s mixed feelings, Hayden Prep had made it out of its first round as well. If both teams won their games tonight, they would meet in the finals, a meeting that T. J. was not looking forward to.

"Uh-oh, I hope this doesn't involve someone named Christopher," T. J. commented as he and Brad entered the den.

"I think you boys had better sit down," their father said seriously.

The brothers exchanged worried glances. "What's up?" Brad asked.

Mr. McKendrick looked at his wife for a moment and then returned his gaze to his sons. "Your mother and I have decided to separate for a while," he said slowly. "It may not be permanent. It's just on a trial basis," he added quickly, seeing the expressions on their faces, "but for now we both feel that . . . it would be the best thing to do."

T. J.'s stomach began to churn.

"But why?" Brad demanded.

"Your mother and I have been having some

problems lately, and we both need to have our space right now," his father said. "I've rented a condo at Crestwood Manor."

T. J. finally found his voice. "Does this mean that you're going to get a divorce?" he asked.

"We both hope it doesn't come to that," Mr. McKendrick replied. "Look, you know that your mother and I haven't been getting along very well lately. And the problems at work have just added to the strain. I hope that the economy will turn around and things will improve at work. Maybe if we can get back on track financially we'll be able to work out some of our other problems."

A horn suddenly blared outside—Steve, Trey, and Russ had arrived—but neither Brad nor T. J. moved.

"Look, I'll always be there for you," their father said. "You know that. Crestwood Manor isn't very far; you can visit whenever you want."

"We know you're upset," Mrs. McKendrick said, "but you've got to try to consider what's best for your father and me too."

"Maybe I don't want to consider what's best for you," Brad snapped.

Mr. McKendrick closed his eyes and then said, "You don't want to keep your friends waiting. Why don't the two of you go ahead to your game now and we'll talk more about this later."

"Right. Thanks for helping us concentrate on the game," Brad said. Giving both his parents a harsh look, he stormed out of the room.

T. J. turned and followed him.

Brad and T. J. hardly spoke during the ten minute trip to the rink, just staring out the window and allowing the other three boys to carry on the conversation. Though Russ and Steve appeared oblivious, Trey kept casting the twins strange glances.

Two hours later both teams were set for the opening face-off. As T. J. waited for the referee to skate out to center ice, he sneaked Brad a look of concern. While T. J. tried to lead more by example, Brad was usually very vocal, giving his teammates advice and doing his best to get them psyched up. But tonight he had barely said two words. "Hey, Brad, keep it in the game tonight, all right?" T. J. said in a low voice. Brad just glared at him and angrily readjusted his helmet.

About ten minutes into the first period, with the Lions up 1–0, T. J. was stick-handling behind Bayview's goal cage when he heard the referee's whistle suddenly chirp irately. Glancing up, T. J. scanned the ice, finally locating two players tussling near the Stoneham blue line. He frowned when he finally caught sight of the Bayview player's number—17. Brad.

"Great, an automatic game misconduct," Trey complained. "I knew something like this was going to happen. He's lucky if he doesn't get thrown out of the tournament."

"So . . . uh, Brad told you?" T. J. asked.

Trey nodded. "Yeah. Listen, my parents split a few years ago, so I know how you guys feel. But maybe things will work out between yours, you know?"

"I hope so," T. J. replied. Returning his eyes to the fight, he saw that Brad had come out the victor. "Well, at least he won," he commented, as the official ripped them apart.

Trey shook his head. "Reynolds doesn't look too thrilled," he observed. He watched as Brad and the Stoneham player headed toward their respective locker rooms. "Brad, man, he's going to be wired."

"Yeah, no kidding," T. J. replied, idly glancing up. He was surprised to see Chris, Jory, and his father there. Mr. McKendrick had just risen from his seat and was elbowing his way down his row, probably on the way to the Bayview locker room. Good luck, Brad, he thought.

"What was that your brother said about letting you guys take care of the scoring, McKendrick?" Glenn McCann asked, skating past him.

"Hey, there's still one of us here, McCann," T. J. replied.

Brad's being thrown out of the game seemed to screw up Bayview's rhythm, but by some miracle they ended up winning, narrowly escaping with a 2–1 victory. Following Brad's fight, Reynolds had moved McCann up to T. J.'s line to take right wing. Until then, T. J. had never realized what a blessing it was playing on a line with his brother; after that first game when they'd refused to play together they had melded perfectly. Glen passed, but never to T. J., almost as if winning the game was less important to him than keeping T. J. from scoring. Nevertheless, T. J. had scored the game-winning goal, but on assists from Steven and Russ. In his mind he had pretended that Stoneham had been on a perpetual power play, and Glen was just one more Lion he had to deal with.

In the locker room, Brad was nowhere to be

seen. He had probably gotten a ride home with Dad, T. J. thought as he took off his skates.

"A very sloppy effort tonight, guys," Coach Reynolds said, striding into the locker room. "If you want the truth, I'm shocked—shocked—that you won. If you had been playing any other team, believe me—you'd be wallowing in self-pity right now. Now, I've just heard that we're going to be going against Hayden Prep in the finals. In case you're at all interested," he added. "They're a tough team, and I'm warning you right now—if you play anything like you did tonight, forget it. And if you did win, it would just be luck, sheer luck, like it was tonight. I don't know about you, but that is not a gamble that I'm willing to take." He fixed them all with a long, hard look, and then disappeared into his office.

"Look, T. J., if you came in here to ream me out, don't bother," Brad said. "It's been done."

T. J. closed Brad's bedroom door. "What's everyone been saying?" he asked.

Brad sighed. "That I'm the captain, and I'm supposed to set an example. That I shirked my responsibility because in a tournament, every game could be our last. I mean, give me a break. It's not like I went out there and said to myself, Gee, I think I'm going to get into a fight tonight. It just happened."

"How did it start?"

"It was stupid," Brad said, shaking his head. "The guy just called me a name or something after I checked him, and I blew up. Usually I don't let stuff like that get to me, but tonight . . ."

T. J. nodded. "How'd you get home?" he wanted to know. "Dad?"

"Yeah."

"What did he say?"

"I don't know, he was okay, I guess. But Chris—Chris was staring daggers at me. I could just hear him remembering all those things I've been telling him about fighting lately."

"Do you think Mom and Dad told them about the separation?"

"Yeah, I guess they must have after we left."

"What about Reynolds? What'd he say?"

"I kind of hinted that I'd been upset before the game, and he said that he understood, but that if I wanted to get anywhere in hockey, I had to learn to separate my 'on-the-ice life from my off-the-ice life.' "

Grinning, T. J. opened the bedroom door. "Deep."

"He must have about had it with me, though," Brad said. "Hey, how'd you like centering for McCann?"

"Let's just say that if you get thrown out of any more games, I'll kill you," T. J. replied. "See you, Brad."

As T. J. left Brad's room and started down the dimly lit hallway, he stopped and paused for a moment outside Chris's door. Yellow light was seeping through the crack at the floor, and low music was vibrating from within. He thought for a moment, and then slowly twisted the knob.

He found Chris sprawled across his bed, his elbows folded behind his head and his eyes fixed on the ceiling. As T. J. stepped in, Chris's eyes flickered toward him for a second, and then quickly jumped back to the ceiling.

"Hi, how're you doing?"

"Fine," Chris said.

"I mean, how are you doing about Mom and Dad?" T. J. asked.

"Okay."

It was like talking to a brick wall, T. J. thought. "So Dad took you to the hockey game, huh?"

Chris nodded.

"Yeah, we played pretty lousy tonight. The coach really gave it to us afterward."

"Oh."

T. J. sighed. "Night, Chris." Shaking his head, he wearily exited the room.

# CHAPTER TWELVE

"MAN, LOOK AT all that snow," Brad marveled the next day, squinting out into the darkness. It was six in the evening, and he and T. J. were in T. J.'s car, driving home from an unusually long hockey practice Reynolds had scheduled in response to their poor performance in the game the day before.

"Did you hear there's supposed to be a big storm tonight?" Brad asked as they approached their street.

"Yeah, but I doubt we'll get it. I have a feeling that by the time we get a big storm, it'll be Christmas vacation, and we'll have the day off anyway."

When they got into the house, they found their parents and Jory in the living room, their father staring vacantly out the window and their mother sitting tearfully on the sofa.

"Hey, what's going on?" T. J. asked.

Mr. McKendrick turned around to face the boys before he spoke. "Christopher . . . he's run away."

Brad's eyes widened. "What? How do you know?"

"Some of his clothes are missing and his coach

said that he skipped practice today," Mrs. McKendrick said. "He must have come home and packed right after school, while I was still at work."

"Did you call the police?" T. J. asked.

His father nodded. "But they said that he hadn't been missing long enough to be cause for alarm. They think he'll come home once the snow starts. But Chris . . . somehow I don't think Chris will give up so easily."

"Which is exactly why you should have insisted that the police start searching for him, Thomas," Mrs. McKendrick snapped.

"Look, Barbara," Mr. McKendrick began impatiently, "what would—"

Mrs. McKendrick just shook her head wearily. "Do either of you have any idea where he might have gone?" she asked Brad and T. J.

T. J. thought for a moment. "No. Did you call all of his friends? All of the kids on the hockey team?"

"Yes, and none of them has seen him since school," his mother told him. "But a couple of them did mention that he seemed upset today."

Something suddenly clicked in Brad's mind. "Wait a minute. . . . I think T. J. and I know where he is," he said.

"We do?" T. J. asked.

"We do. Look, give us an hour, okay?" he told his parents. "Don't do anything until around seven o'clock."

Hope gleamed in Mrs. McKendrick's eyes. "Where he is . . . do you think he's okay?" she asked anxiously.

I hope so, Brad thought to himself. "Yeah. I'm sure he's fine," he reassured her.

"Where do you think he is?" T. J. asked a few minutes later as he started his car.

"Silver Creek."

"Do you really think he's there?"

"Well, that's where I'd go," Brad said. "Chris and I are so much alike. I can usually figure out what he's thinking."

T. J. felt an unexpected twinge of jealousy. "Remember when we were kids—we used to be able to practically read each other's minds."

"We still can, sometimes," Brad replied. "Like on the ice. It's almost like we're the same person. It makes us play even better, I think."

"Yeah. I'd forgotten how great it feels, that closeness."

They drove in silence for a while, then Brad spoke. "Look," he said. "I'm sorry about the way I treated you when you first started at Bayview. It was just hard for me, having to share the spotlight, especially in hockey."

"I'd have felt the same way," T. J. told him. "But it was hard for me, too. I was riding pretty high at Hayden. It was tough being the new kid."

"I guess I should have understood that," Brad responded.

"I should have seen your side too," T. J. replied. "Anyway, I still miss Hayden but . . . I'm glad I have the chance to play with you. And to sort of get to know you better."

Brad smiled. "Me too."

Fifteen minutes later when they finally arrived

at Silver Creek, the air was thick with twirling dots of snow.

"I hope he has enough sense not to climb those rocks," T. J. said, pulling open his car door. "With all that ice . . ."

"Don't worry. Chris is a tough kid." But Brad sounded pretty worried himself.

"I guess," T. J. said.

Jamming his hands into the pockets of his Bayview jacket, Brad stepped out of the car. "If he is here, the snow's probably erased all his footprints by now," he commented grimly.

Despite the raw scraping wind and the furiously whipping snowflakes, Silver Creek appeared oddly serene, the velvety blackness of night a stark contrast to the soft white blanket of snow. Tall trees loomed high in the distance, throwing moving shadows across the glittering stretch of ice.

T. J. cupped his hands around his mouth. "Chris! Christopher!" he shouted. He waited, but the only reply that greeted him was his own echo.

"Christopher! Christopher!" Brad yelled, glancing around. Sighing, he turned to T. J. "We're so stupid. Why didn't we bring a flashlight?"

They had been combing the area beneath the rocks for about five minutes when T. J. suddenly said, "Wait a minute. We are being stupid. Where don't you want to be in the middle of a snowstorm?"

Brad nodded. "Outside."

"Exactly," T. J. said.

Stepping up onto the rocks, they carefully climbed upward, angry snowflakes stinging their cheeks and making their eyes water. They peered

**107**

into cave after cave, and just as Brad was beginning to think they'd never find Chris, T. J. yelled in relief. "Brad! Here he is!"

As Brad quickly scrambled into the cave after his brother, he saw Chris leaning against the back wall, his body bunched in thick layers of clothing, and a small fire crackling on the floor before him. The flames cast eerie shadows on the dank walls, all flickering and wavering, like a candle.

Brad's relief turned to anger. "Christopher, do you know how worried everyone's been about you?" he demanded fiercely. "It's the middle of a blizzard, for God's sake. You've got everyone scared to death."

"How did you find me?" Chris asked.

"Great minds think alike," Brad replied. He knelt down in front of the fire. "Chris, another day and they would have had your face on the side of a milk carton. We know you're upset about Mom and Dad, but it's upsetting for them too, and you're just making it harder for everyone."

"Yeah, but ..." Looking downcast, Chris stopped and gazed listlessly into the fire.

Brad glanced at T. J. "But what?" he asked gently.

Chris hesitated. "Well, I thought ... maybe if they thought I'd run away or something, they'd get worried and ... get back together."

T. J. sighed. "Chris, they're not going to get back together. At least not right away. You've got to face that, just like I've got to face that Dad's never going to accept my not wanting to be a lawyer."

"There're some things you just can't change," Brad said.

"So . . . it didn't work then?" Chris murmured.

Brad leaned forward and squeezed his younger brother's shoulder. "Sorry, Chris, but the last we saw, they were arguing."

"Look, this thing with Mom and Dad has been tough on all of us," T. J. said, "but, Chris, you've got to pull yourself out of this."

"Come on, Chris, you can't leave me alone with T. J. and Jory," Brad implored. "Who am I going to have a decent conversation with?"

A small grin began to tug on Chris's lips.

"Come on, kid," Brad said. "Let's go home."


The next day, Brad arrived at psychology class early. He took a deep breath and approached Sherry's desk. "Hi, Sherry."

Smiling, she glanced up from her notebook. "Hi, Brad," she said. "Are you ready for the quiz?"

"Not really. Are you?"

"Well, I hope so. But I don't know though."

"Look, I was wondering . . . would you want to go to a movie with me this Saturday?" Brad asked.

"That sounds good," Sherry said. "Why don't you call me Saturday morning with the schedule."

"Yeah, sure."

Her smile wider now, she scribbled her number down onto a sheet of notebook paper. "Here you go," she said, tearing it out. "You can call me before Saturday if you'd like."

Brad nodded. "I'll give you a call tonight."

"Okay."

"Well, good luck on the quiz."

"You too," Sherry said. "I'll talk to you later, Brad."

Brad's smile faded as he turned around and saw Trey and T. J. grinning at him from the back of the room. He headed toward them reluctantly. "What?"

T. J. and Trey looked at each other. "Nothing," T. J. replied.

"What?" Brad demanded.

"Did we say anything?"

Shaking his head, Brad sat down.

"So you finally put the moves on her, huh, ace?" Trey asked, smirking.

"Did she say yes?" T. J. asked.

Brad grinned at them. "What do you think?"

"Gee, man, I'm sorry," T. J. said.

Trey burst out laughing.

"You jerk." Brad pushed his desk into T. J.'s, and then grinning again, faced front.

The atmosphere in the locker room was quiet, and the players, all dressing, were speaking in hushed monotones. When Brad had finished lacing his skates, he pulled on his blue jersey with the white captain's "C" emblazoned on the front and B. McKendrick and the number 17 on the back. As he carefully adjusted it over his shoulder pads and elbow guards, he felt a heavy hand clap down on his arm. Brad glanced up into the doughy face of Coach Reynolds.

"No rough stuff out there tonight, got it, kid?" Reynolds asked.

Brad smiled sheepishly. "Got it, coach," he replied, rummaging around in his duffel bag.

Nodding, Reynolds strode to the center of the locker room. "Okay, guys, Hayden's major strength is that they're always hustling. They're going to be throwing body checks like crazy, and they're not going to give up without a fight. But if you stay on your toes and play like you're capable of playing, then you've got yourself a tournament crown. And remember what T. J. told you. If they've got McPherson in goal tonight, try shooting upstairs, because that was his major weakness last year. Now I want to see some communication out there. Remember, when you're on that ice, you're a family, a unit. Talk to each other, and don't be afraid to give each other advice." He smacked his hands together. "Now let's go get ourselves a trophy."

A thrill of excitement rippled through the crowd as the teams emerged from the darkness of the runway and streamed onto the brilliantly illuminated ice. Brad glanced up into the stands, and saw Sherry waving to him eagerly. A couple of rows up from her were his mother and Chris and Jory. Jessica winked at him from the large circle of cheerleaders on the sidelines, and grinning, Brad winked back.

Trey and the Hayden goalie, Tim McPherson, skated toward their respective cages, bulky in their heavy pads and swaying as they moved. The Jets, resplendent in royal blue and bright white, and the Rockets, in red and white, swung around their own halves of the ice as they began their pregame warm-ups.

A few moments later, as the national anthem ended and the referee tooted on his whistle for the opening face-off, Brad glanced at T. J., and T. J. rolled his eyes at him. It was obvious that T. J. was tense, and Brad had to sympathize with him; playing against one's old teammates had to be awful. Facing off against Kevin something, who Brad recognized as a good friend of his brother's, T. J. leaned forward, firmly planting his stick to the ice.

Kevin suddenly smiled. "Hey, McKendrick! I don't want to say good luck, so I'll just say don't trip over the blue line or anything, okay?"

T. J. smiled back. "Likewise, but don't think I'm not gonna smash you into the boards a few times, Mattrex."

"Better not. I've still got your Aerosmith tape."

As the referee dropped the puck between the two opposing centers, the huge clock poised above center ice began to tick off the seconds. T. J. pounced on the disk, and slid it across the ice to Brad. The right winger promptly swooped over the blue line and into Rocket territory, heading for the Hayden goal cage. Two defensemen bumped into him, one from each side, and Brad fell down between them. The puck skittered harmlessly toward goalkeeper McPherson, who crept out of the net and slapped it into the corner.

"T. J., pass it!" Brad yelled a few moments later, as he swerved around a burly defenseman. Automatically, T. J. sent the puck sailing over to him, and the rubber immediately latched onto Brad's stuck. Looping in closer to the net, he flicked his wrist, and with a determined set to his chin flipped the puck upstairs, over the goalie's left shoulder. As the Bayview fans erupted into cheers, McPherson slammed down his stick and began muttering under his breath, all the while casting Brad ferocious glances.

A few minutes later, Hayden tied it up, on a power-play goal by Justin Alexander; the Jets' Brett Hawkins had been taken out for hooking. Exchanging grim looks with T. J., Brad vaulted over the boards for a line change.

The Rocket center got the draw on the next face-off and richocheted the puck off the sideboard toward the blue line. Brian Harper, Hayden's senior defenseman, skated in from his position on left point and fired a slap shot on goal. Trey batted it out and directed it toward T. J., who shot the puck the length of the ice.

The first period ended in a 1–1 tie, and most of the second period was uneventful. However, with only forty seconds remaining in the second, Kevin executed a perfect lead pass to left winger Blake Anderson. Blake broke around defenseman Russ McRae and tore down the right lane, causing Trey to move out of the net slowly to cut down on the shooting angle. From nearly twenty feet out, Blake unleashed a terrific slap shot toward a small corner of the net. The disk slipped between Trey's goalie pads and over the goal line, lifting the score to Hayden 2, Bayview 1. Five seconds later, the buzzer sounded, ending the second period of play. The disheartened Jets filed into the locker room.

"Look, you've still got an entire period to go," Reynolds said, as the team slumped onto the bench. "A lot can happen in that time." He paused, as Coach Ryan began passing out trays of orange slices. "But I will tell you one thing. I don't like the vibes I'm picking up here. You guys are letting them steal away your confidence. You're the better team. Remember that." He cleared his throat. "Now, you kids have got a real battle on your hands. To win this, you've got to go out there and hustle one hundred and ten percent. In this next period, we really need to shake up some offense, so Russ, I'm going to take you off defense for a while and put in an extra forward, who will be Mike. You'll move up to take Mike's place on the second line with Glen and Tony." He pulled open the door and said, "Get out there and play some hockey!" As his team began to pile out of the locker room and up the ramp leading to the rink, Reynolds motioned over to Brad and T. J.

"Ordinarily I wouldn't tell you this until after the game was completed," Reynolds began, "but I think this just might give you the lift that you guys need. A couple of weeks ago, I heard a friend of mine, a scout for an NHL expansion team, was going to be in town this week on business, so I gave him a call and told him to drop by the tournament if he had a chance, to take a look at you two. Coach Ryan just told me that the guy is up in the stands. Lucky for killer over there he didn't decide to come to the last game," he added wryly, looking at Brad. "Now if you can impress him tonight, believe me, he'll be keeping a very sharp eye on you in the future. You two are doing fine as it is, but if you use what I've just told you to inspire yourselves, and to dig deep within yourselves, you may just go out there and score another goal or two." He shook hands with both of them and then disappeared up the ramp.

Brad and T. J. stared at each other. "Did he just say what I think he said?" Brad asked.

"I don't believe this. They had to pick tonight? My worst game of the season? What kind of odds is that?"

"Your worst game of the season? What about me?"

"Yeah, you're doing terrible, Brad. You just happened to score our only goal," T. J. said.

"Well, you heard the man. Let's do it." They slapped high fives, and then skated onto the ice. The Bayview fans, and even some of T. J.'s friends in the Hayden crowd, clapped wildly at the sight of them.

The third period opened with a frenzy. Still trailing by one goal, the Jets fought desperately to control the puck in the Rocket end of the ice. When the Rockets got it, they would promptly shoot it out, and then the Jets would form up at center ice and carry it again.

"Come on, Glen, dig it out!" Reynolds shouted from behind the bench. "Bring it up!"

With six minutes remaining in the game, and Hayden still leading 2 to 1, Brad dashed across the blue line, cut over to the center from his right wing position, and left a drop pass for T. J. Using Brad as a screen, T. J. thundered a hard shot on the Rockets' goal. At the last second, McPherson kicked it out, but Brad, not missing a beat, caught the disk on his stick and slid it over to T. J., who in turn thrust it into an open corner of the net.

"All right! Nice shot!" Brad said enthusiastically, pounding his brother's shoulders.

"Thanks. Nice assist," T. J. responded, grinning crookedly. "Think that's what Reynolds meant?"

The next five minutes were extremely tense, one moment all the action in the Jet's zone, and the next in the Rockets'. There were twenty seconds remaining in regulation when Brad suddenly broke away from the shadow that Hayden had pinned on him, first feigning one way, and then the other. Carrying the puck on his stick, he whipped across the blue line, like a blue and white streak of lightning. As he got in closer, he faked to the left, drawing McPherson out and to one side. He then pulled the puck back, drew his stick to the right, and flipped the puck backhanded into the open net. A split second after the red light flashed on, the final buzzer clanged, sending Brad's teammates pouring around him and pummeling him excitedly.

"Well, you always were dramatic," T. J. commented.

As the words "Bayview goal by number seventeen . . . Brad McKendrick," boomed over the loudspeaker, T. J. disappeared for a moment, returning a second later with the game-winning puck. "Here. Someone once told me it was for luck."

Brad smiled. "Smart person," he said, accepting it. "You in the mood to meet a scout?"

T. J. laughed. "After I take a shower maybe. You in the mood to accept a trophy?"

Brad grinned. "Yeah, I suppose I could settle for that." Slapping gloves, they merged into the circle of their teammates, on their way to accept their trophy.

STACY DRUMTRA lives with her family in Massachusetts, where she attends college. An avid Bruins fan, she also enjoys tennis and exercising, and has been writing since elementary school.

# TERRIFYING TALES OF
# SPINE-TINGLING SUSPENSE

## THE MAN WHO WAS POE          Avi
71192-3/$3.99 US/$4.99 Can

Is the mysterious stranger really the tormented writer Edgar Allan Poe, looking to use Edmund's plight as the source of a new story—with a tragic ending?

## DYING TO KNOW          Jeff Hammer
76143-2/$3.50 US/$4.50 Can

When Diane Delany investigates the death of her sworn enemy, she uncovers many dark secrets and begins to wonder if she can trust anyone—even her boyfriend.

## FIELD TRIP          Jeff Hammer
76144-0/$2.99 US/$3.50 Can

On a weekend field trip, Tom Martin doesn't know who to turn to when students start disappearing, leaving behind only their blood-spattered beds.

## ALONE IN THE HOUSE          Edmund Plante
76424-5/$3.50 US/$4.50 Can

In the middle of the night Joanne wakes up all alone... almost.

## ON THE DEVIL'S COURT          Carl Deuker
70879-5/$3.50 US/$4.50 Can

Desperate for one perfect basketball season, Joe Faust will sacrifice anything for triumph... even his soul.

# NOVELS FROM AVON FLARE

| CLASS PICTURES | 61408-1/$2.95 US/$3.50 Can |
|---|---|

**Marilyn Sachs**

Pat, always the popular one, and shy, plump Lolly have been best friends since kindergarten, through thick and thin, supporting each other during crises. But everything changes when Lolly turns into a thin, pretty blonde and Pat finds herself playing second fiddle for the first time.

| BABY SISTER | 70358-1/$3.50 US/$4.25 Can |
|---|---|

**Marilyn Sachs**

Her sister was everything Penny could never be, until Penny found something else.

| THE GROUNDING OF GROUP 6 | 83386-7/$3.99 US/$4.99 Can |
|---|---|

**Julian Thompson**

What do parents do when they realize that their sixteen-year old son or daughter is a loser and an embarrassment to the family? Five misfits find they've been set up to disappear at exclusive Coldbrook School, but aren't about to allow themselves to be permanently "grounded."

| TAKING TERRI MUELLER | 79004-1/$3.50 US/$4.25 Can |
|---|---|

**Norma Fox Mazer**

Was it possible to be kidnapped by your own father? Terri's father has always told her that her mother died in a car crash—but now Terri has reason to suspect differently, and she struggles to find the truth on her own.

| WHEN DOES THE FUN START? | 76129-7/$3.50 US/$4.25 Can |
|---|---|

**Jean Thesman**

Nothing has been any fun for Teddy Gideon since she spotted Zack, the love of her life, gazing into the eyes of another girl—a beautiful girl Teddy has never seen before.

---

Buy these books at your local bookstore or use this coupon for ordering:

Mail to: Avon Books, Dept BP, Box 767, Rte 2, Dresden, TN 38225          B
Please send me the book(s) I have checked above.
☐ My check or money order—no cash or CODs please—for $_____ is enclosed (please add $1.50 to cover postage and handling for each book ordered—Canadian residents add 7% GST).
☐ Charge my VISA/MC Acct#_____ Exp Date_____
Phone No_____ Minimum credit card order is $6.00 (please add postage and handling charge of $2.00 plus 50 cents per title after the first two books to a maximum of six dollars—Canadian residents add 7% GST). For faster service, call 1-800-762-0779. Residents of Tennessee, please call 1-800-633-1607. Prices and numbers are subject to change without notice. Please allow six to eight weeks for delivery.

Name_____

Address_____

City_____ State/Zip_____

FLB 0292

## Spine-tingling Suspense
## from Avon Flare

# JAY BENNETT

**THE EXECUTIONER**                     79160-9/$2.95 US/3.50 Can

Indirectly responsible for a friend's death, Bruce is consumed by guilt—until someone is out to get *him*.

# CHRISTOPHER PIKE

**CHAIN LETTER**                     89968-X/$3.99 US/$4.99 Can

One by one, the chain letter was coming to each of them... demanding dangerous, impossible deeds. None in the group wanted to believe it—until the accidents—and the dying—started happening!

# NICOLE DAVIDSON

**WINTERKILL**                     75965-9/$2.95 US/$3.50 Can

Her family's move to rural Vermont proves dangerous for Karen Henderson as she tries to track down the killer of her friend Matt.

**CRASH COURSE**                     75964-0/$3.50 US/$4.25 Can

A secluded cabin on the lake was a perfect place to study...or to die.

# Avon Books presents
# your worst nightmares—

## ...gut-wrenching terror

**BY BIZARRE HANDS**

71205-9/$3.99 US/$4.99 Can

Joe R. Lansdale

**THE ARCHITECTURE OF FEAR**

70553-2/$3.95 US/$4.95 Can

edited by Kathryn Cramer & Peter D. Pautz

## ...unspeakable evil

**COLD SHOCKS**     76160-2/$4.50 US/$5.50 Can
edited by Tim Sullivan

**EYES OF NIGHT**    76011-8/$3.95 US/$4.95 Can
David C. Smith

## ...blood lust

**THE HUNGER**      70441-2/$4.99 US/$5.99 Can
**THE WOLFEN**      70440-4/$4.50 US/$5.95 Can
Whitley Strieber